He Gazed Into Her Eyes

then gently, ever so gently, he lifted her chin to tilt her face up to his. His lips came down on hers, the touch cool, firm, and Amanda felt a sweet aching throughout her whole being, spinning her heart and senses and sending the blood rushing hotly through her veins. She clung to him, wanting desperately to forget everything, everything but this magic moment of love. . . .

D1320487

More Romance from SIGNET

☐ ROMANCE IN THE HEADLINES by Mary Ann TAYLOR.   (#W7439—$1.50)

☐ A VOTE FOR LOVE by Arlene Hale.
(#Y7505—$1.25)

☐ LEGACY OF LOVE by Arlene Hale.
(#W7411—$1.50)

☐ THE HEART REMEMBERS by Arlene Hale.
(#Q6817—95¢)

☐ IN LOVE'S OWN FASHION by Arlene Hale.
(#Y6846—$1.25)

☐ THE KEY TO HER HEART by Julia Alcott.
(#Y7103—$1.25)

☐ A LONG LOST LOVE by Julia Alcott.
(#Y7190—$1.25)

☐ HER HEART'S DESIRE by Lynna Cooper.
(#Q6913—95¢)

☐ FOLLOW THE HEART by Heather Sinclair.
(#Q6845—95¢)

☐ SIGNET DOUBLE ROMANCE—THE ALIEN HEART by Alice Lent Covert and MAKE WAY FOR SPRING by Peggy O'More.   (#W7191—$1.50)

☐ SIGNET DOUBLE ROMANCE—A CONFLICT OF WOMEN by Emma Darby and HAVEN OF PEACE by I. Torr.   (#W7370—$1.50)

☐ SIGNET DOUBLE ROMANCE—SHEILA'S DILEMMA by Ivy Valdes and THE INTRUSION by Elizabeth McCrae.   (#W7440—$1.50)

THE NEW AMERICAN LIBRARY, INC.,
P.O. Box 999, Bergenfield, New Jersey 07621

Please send me the SIGNET BOOKS I have checked above. I am enclosing $_____(check or money order—no currency or C.O.D.'s). Please include the list price plus 35¢ a copy to cover handling and mailing costs. (Prices and numbers are subject to change without notice.)

Name_____

Address_____

City_____State_____Zip Code_____
Allow at least 4 weeks for delivery

Bon Voyage, My Darling

By MARY ANN TAYLOR

A SIGNET BOOK

NEW AMERICAN LIBRARY

TIMES MIRROR

NAL BOOKS ARE ALSO AVAILABLE AT DISCOUNTS IN BULK
QUANTITY FOR INDUSTRIAL OR SALES-PROMOTIONAL
USE. FOR DETAILS, WRITE TO PREMIUM MARKETING
DIVISION, NEW AMERICAN LIBRARY, INC., 1301 AVENUE
OF THE AMERICAS, NEW YORK, NEW YORK 10019.

COPYRIGHT © 1977 BY MARY ANN TAYLOR

All rights reserved

 SIGNET TRADEMARK REG. U.S. PAT. OFF. AND FOREIGN COUNTRIES
REGISTERED TRADEMARK—MARCA REGISTRADA
HECHO EN CHICAGO, U.S.A.

SIGNET, SIGNET CLASSICS, MENTOR, PLUME AND
MERIDIAN BOOKS
are published by The New American Library, Inc.,
1301 Avenue of the Americas, New York, New York 10019

FIRST SIGNET PRINTING, JULY, 1977

1 2 3 4 5 6 7 8 9

PRINTED IN THE UNITED STATES OF AMERICA

Chapter 1

Amanda Conklin, trim in her new dark-blue pantsuit, tawny blond hair blowing in the ocean breeze, followed the broad shoulders of the baggageman up the gangway of the cruise ship. They crossed the deck, elbowed through the crowded foyer, and went down a long, brilliantly polished passageway to halt before a room at the end of a hall.

The baggageman shifted his load slightly, glanced up at the number, then craned his head back over his shoulder. "You did say number 224, right?"

Amanda consulted the paper she held in her hand. "Right."

He nodded, pushed open the door, and lumbered inside to begin unloading her suitcases onto the floor. Amanda was about to follow, but before she could enter the room, the door across the way opened and a young man came out, hesitated the briefest of seconds to give her a swift admiring glance, then greeted her politely before striding off down the hall. She had the fleeting impression of a tweed-jacketed individual, tall and brown-haired, with alert gray eyes.

Amanda smiled to herself. The cruise looked promising indeed, if her new neighbor proved to be an example of the newly boarding passengers.

Stepping inside her room, she pressed back against the door to avoid interfering with the placing of the

1

suitcases. Glancing about quickly, she realized the room was small, very small indeed. Not a lot of space for one, certainly a snug fit for two, but it would do, she thought approvingly, it would do!

Her eager eyes took in the long built-in dressing table that ran along the wall to her right, with twin sets of drawers, one at each end, one for her roommate, one for her. Above the dressing table, a large square mirror reflected back her oval face with cheeks flushed with excitement. To her left, a narrow blue sofa that no doubt made up into a bed at night; above it, a bunk that folded into the wall. And that was it, the entire stateroom, except for the two small closets and a half-open door revealing the compact bathroom.

For the next six weeks she would be sharing this undeniably snug room with her future roommate. Amanda paused, frowning. What would she be like, this other girl? She had no idea, she knew only that she could never have afforded the expense of a single room. Amanda sighed. Heaven prevent the newcomer from being a problem type! But she resolved then and there that she would not allow anyone to spoil this trip. It meant too much to her.

Abruptly she was aware of a throat being cleared. She looked up to see the baggageman, his work completed, gazing at her with expectant eyes. Hurriedly she dug into her purse to hand him a tip. Giving her a nod and lifting his hand to touch his cap politely, he broke into a grin. "Sure hope you have a nice trip, miss." He backed out through the open door, then went on down the hall.

Amanda hoped it would be a good trip, too. She stood for a moment, purse still clasped in her hands, as the memory of Mr. Leland's frown and grudging permission to finally allow her the time off rose vividly in her mind.

"Nonsense, pure poppycock!" he had snapped, glowering at her over his glasses. "Sentimental journey ... ridiculous waste of time and money!" Then he had called to her as she started out of his office, "And see that you are back here on time, it's enough of an inconvenience as it is."

But here she was. It had taken nearly two years to arrange and had wiped out her bank account, right down to twenty-seven cents. Well, she thought excitedly, she wasn't going to miss one moment of it!

Whirling about, she picked up one of the two door keys on the dressing table and hurried out, back down the passageway, edging around incoming passengers and struggling baggage handlers.

Up on deck, she halted to look about for an instant, then moved over to the railing, leaning over to watch the other people boarding, wondering whimsically if she could possibly pick out her future roommate. Hopefully not that petulant redhead who was already ordering stewards about in that irritated, carrying voice. Amanda watched as the newcomer tossed a scathing look at the other travelers, obviously weighing them in her mind, then clearly not finding them to her taste, for she tossed her head arrogantly and disappeared into the ship's foyer.

Bon-voyage groups gathered about in noisy, laughing clusters. For an instant a little touch of loneliness swept over her. She had come from the southwest, too far for anyone to be here to see her off on the trip. Then she smiled, the feeling gone as she touched the lei of frangipani blossoms around her neck, the very motion sending a stir of fragrance floating up. From the group at work, not from Mr. Leland, of course, but from her fellow workers who knew how much this trip meant to her.

Amanda stood watching until the blast of the ship's whistle and repeated cries of all ashore had sent visitors scurrying down the gangway. An orchestra on board struck up farewell music and a steward began moving among the passengers, handing out colored serpentine to be tossed, twirling and unwinding, down at the people waving good-bye and calling last farewells from the dock.

Slowly the great ship began pulling away, heading out into the bay and out to the open sea.

It was beginning! Turning quickly, she hurried to the stern to take a last long look at San Francisco. The sun was setting and a copper glow spread over the hills, glinting into the windows like a million blazing fires.

The view suddenly blurred before her eyes. Overlaying all the excitement of making the trip was the poignancy of going all by herself. There had been such glorious plans for the three of them, her mother and father should have been with her, if things hadn't suddenly gone to pieces and her young world fallen around her. As long as she could remember, her parents had spoken, not only spoken . . . planned . . . on taking this cruise to the South Pacific. On their twenty-fifth anniversary. And her twenty-first birthday. They had gone on the same voyage on their honeymoon.

But all those plans had ended, abruptly, tragically, when the small two-engined plane they were riding in with friends crashed into the Grand Canyon. She had been fourteen. A maiden aunt, her father's sister, had grudgingly given her a home until she was out of high school and could support herself.

Sentimental? With the back of her hand she wiped the tears away. Of course she was. She was taking the trip now, the trip they had always wanted to make again. Mr. Leland had at first refused her the time off. But she had given up her vacation two years in a row, which gave her four weeks, and she had trained a girl to take her place and had to pay her for those two precious extra weeks. Mr. Leland hadn't been happy about it, he hated having office routine changed for any reason, he simply couldn't understand why his secretary was going to absent herself for six whole weeks on such a ridiculous, expensive errand.

Expensive? That it was, she reflected. How she had scrimped, done without everything except the most necessary of things, never once touching the small amount of insurance money that had been her inheritance. But she had put it all together, and here she was, just two months past her twenty-first birthday.

"Hello, neighbor! The San Francisco skyline is quite a sight, isn't it? Unforgettable!"

Amanda was aware of a tweed-sleeved arm on the railing beside her. She turned to look up into the face of the man from across the hall.

"Yes, it certainly . . ." she began, then her voice halted as she realized he was staring down at her, his eyebrows arched in surprise.

"Good lord, your eyes are green! Not just green, but the exact shade of emeralds." Suddenly he was apologetic. "I'm sorry, I had no intention of being rude, but I'm an artist and I've never seen eyes quite like yours." He peered closer. "They are absolutely unusual." Then he grinned. "There I go, apologizing one minute and starting all over the next."

Amanda wasn't sure if he had noticed the wetness of her lashes, but if he did, he gave no sign of it. She found it difficult to know how to reply to such exuberant comment, so she contented herself with a smile.

They returned their attention to the silhouette of the vanishing city turning dark against a background of orange-spattered clouds.

"Are you from San Francisco?" he asked.

"No, from Arizona." Amanda was watching the starkly outlined buildings, small lights beginning to appear like stars in some of them.

They chatted idly, exchanging names, wandering lazily through the usual shipboard small talk. He was Graham Moore, he told her, from Trenton, New Jersey, and this was his second trip to the South Pacific.

"I only hope it is as wonderful as I've always dreamed it was, Tahiti, Fiji, all those other South Sea islands." Even saying their names sent a ripple of excitement up her spine.

He smiled at her indulgently, his gray eyes amused. "You lit up like a thousand lights when you said that, Amanda. Mind if I call you Amanda?" At her nod of consent, he continued, "You can be assured that it is, every bit as enchanting and exciting as you have read ... or dreamed about."

They were passing under Golden Gate Bridge, its spires pushing up into the soft puffs of fog that had begun to descend. The wind caught Amanda's hair, blowing it across her face. She lifted a hand to brush it back and looked up to see Graham Moore regarding her with more than casual interest.

She turned away, feeling a warm flush of her cheeks. He was certainly attentive for such short acquaintance, she reflected, not exactly displeased.

They watched as the dusk began softening, then erasing the shoreline. The small pilot boat left them and went chugging back to port.

"You missed it, there goes your last chance to abandon ship," he said, nodding toward the boat that had now nearly disappeared.

"I plan to stay. It's taken me long enough to get this far and I'm not going to leave this cruise until we dock back in San Francisco, six weeks from now." She laughed, then shivered slightly, feeling the bite of the wind through her jacket.

"You're cold." He bent over her attentively, his arm brushing hers. "Wouldn't you like to go inside and I'll see about getting us a cup of coffee, or a drink if you'd rather?"

This was all moving along just a little faster than she'd really prefer, Amanda decided. Not that he wasn't a most attractive man, or his attention displeasing, but there'd be plenty of time ahead to become better acquainted. She didn't want to become too involved with one particular person this early in the trip.

"Thanks, but I'd really better get down to my stateroom. I'd like to meet my roommate and unpack," she said.

"Ah, ha!" He laughed triumphantly. "Now that's what I've been trying to extract from you in my most adroit and, up until now, unsuccessful way. I wanted to find out if this was an unattached, attractive young woman, or if there might also be an accompanying encumbrance in the way of a husband. I know from experience that good-looking girls are not in oversupply on these trips and the competition can get pretty tough, both from the ship's personnel and the other passengers. So I'm openly declaring I'm putting in my bid early."

Amanda couldn't help laughing. "I must say you don't waste time. And, I assure you, there's no—what did you call it—accompanying encumbrance. No husband."

They walked together in through the doors past a large salon and onto a stairway leading below to the rooms. The halls were nearly empty now. Here and there a half-open door revealed the remnants of a bon-voyage party. At Amanda's stateroom Graham paused. "See you a little later?"

"On board ship? How can you miss?" she replied airily. "Even if you wanted to!"

She fitted her key into the door, raised a few fingers in a quick farewell to him, and stepped inside her stateroom.

Her roommate had arrived. Three suitcases, added to

her own not inconsiderable luggage, made the room barely navigable. There was no evidence of the girl, but the sound of a shower furnished the clue to her whereabouts. Putting her key back into her purse, Amanda stepped over one of the stranger's bags to look at the name tag. Wynne Harrison, New York City.

She sat down on the sofa, kicking off her shoes, waiting for the appearance of her roommate so they could settle who should have which bed and which set of drawers.

Her mind drifted back to Graham and those cheerfully exuberant compliments, nine-tenths of which he surely couldn't mean. Still, even if it was all in fun, it did wonders for a girl's morale.

The sound of the shower dwindled, then shut off. For a few moments there was silence. Suddenly the bathroom door opened.

Standing in the doorway was a tall young man, hair wet, clad only in a towel wrapped insecurely around his waist.

Amanda's eyes flew wide. "*What are you doing in my room?*" she hurled her voice angrily at the bathroom door, which had slammed shut abruptly.

There was silence, then the door opened a few inches and a pair of startled eyes peered out through the crack. "Madam, I am not in your room, you are in mine. I would appreciate your leaving at once."

Amanda stiffened. "*I?* This is my room. It is 224, I was assigned to 224. Will you kindly remove yourself—clothed, if you don't mind? Otherwise, I shall call the steward to see that you're forcibly escorted out!" She stared back at the eyes indignantly.

There was a slight pause while the man seemed to be considering his next move. Then he said, with massive dignity, "If you will please hand me that brown overnight case, I shall be dressed in a moment. I need a clean shirt and a pair of pants; my others, unfortunately, are in the closet."

Exasperated, she bent over to pick up the bag, then halted to look up uncertainly, "You, you are Wynne Harrison?" Her voice rose incredulously.

The eyes flicked with what looked like complacency, maybe even triumph. "I am."

"But you are not my ... my roommate, Wynne Harrison?" she said, completely confused. This was ridiculous!

"I certainly do happen to be Wynne Harris—" His head jerked, dark eyebrows flying up over indignant blue eyes. "For the love of Pete, I'll say I'm not your roommate!"

She lifted the bag numbly and handed it to him. A bare arm extended gingerly to take it, then maneuvered it cautiously through the narrow door opening. The door shut.

Amanda sank down on the sofa. This was preposterous. One thing she was certain of: she was not going to stir a foot out of this room until the mix-up was settled. He should be the one to go, it was not his room. She and her roommate— Startled, she looked about her. Her real roommate, where was she?

Amanda bit at her lips nervously, a very unpleasant suspicion beginning to creep into the back of her mind. She stared at the bathroom door. It couldn't be; it was some gross mistake ... surely ... something!

Slowly the bathroom door opened wide and the annoyed-faced young man came out. He was clothed, all right, in a casual pair of slacks and gray sport shirt. Black Irish, she thought instinctively, for he had the appearance of a certain type of Irishman: dark crisply curling hair, eyes of a startling blue, thick lashed, and a firm expressive mouth. Right now the mouth was expressing irritation.

"I'm sorry for your inconvenience"—his voice was rigidly polite—"but contrary to your opinion, I am not in the wrong stateroom. May I suggest you consult your ticket and examine it more closely?" He stepped over to the closet and took a wallet from a jacket pocket, extracting a piece of paper. "Here is my room assignment."

Amanda gingerly leaned forward to look, lifted her eyes quickly to glance at him, then back again to the paper. She swallowed hard, reaching slowly for her purse.

"Well, am I right?" He spoke quietly now, with all the self-assurance of having won the argument.

She opened her purse, withdrawing her reservation without a word, and handed it to him.

"I'll be damned!" he exploded. "Someone's made one hell of a mistake. These are both for 224."

"Then," she said sweetly, "I'm afraid you'll have to find yourself another room."

He frowned, looking thoughtful, but still completely cool. "I'll tell you what I'll do. I heard this ship had been oversold, but why don't I check right away to see if there is another room available with a single person in it, another woman who might be alone. That would resolve the problem, wouldn't it?"

Or a single man in one, she thought fleetingly, wondering why he hadn't included that, but she said, "Very well, I'm certain that would be the most logical thing to do." Suddenly repentant and a bit embarrassed, she added, "I'm sorry I shouted at you, but I was startled."

He grinned, his eyes crinkling in a fan of small wrinkles. "I don't blame you. I might say I was pretty stunned myself to almost walk in on an attractive stranger in little more than my birthday suit." She saw a tinge of color at the tip of his ears.

"I'll go right now to see the purser and find out what can be done." He was heading for the door. "Will you be waiting here?"

Possession is nine points of the law, she reflected. "Yes, I'll be here, in case someone else shows up to move in with either of us."

"Heaven forbid," he said wryly. "It shouldn't take long for the purser to run through the list. It may take a little longer to get someone to shove over, but these rooms are sold with that understanding, of doubling up, I guess. Unless you want to pay extra for a single?"

"Oh, no," she gasped. "I can't. I mean, I—well, a shared room is all I can afford."

"Don't worry, we'll work it out." He gave her a reassuring nod and left.

Amanda leaned back against the sofa as she sank down on it. She didn't know whether to be dismayed or amused. They would surely get it straightened out. She refused to worry. Suddenly she giggled. Oh, dear, that Wynne Harrison had looked positively paralyzed when he yanked open the bathroom door and found her in the stateroom. Wait until she told her friends back home about it!

Thinking of her friends made her wonder if the girl she had trained to take her place would work out. Mr. Leland had almost conditioned himself not to be satisfied with her. But Amanda knew the girl could do as well as she could herself, so she refused to worry about it anymore, nor would she worry about the mix-up on the room. This was her once-in-a-lifetime dream and nothing was going to spoil it!

She let her eyes roam idly about the room. There was a small card folded over, propped on the dressing table and labeled WELCOME ABOARD. She picked it up to read while she waited. Tips on how to avoid shipboard mishaps, hours of meals—her eyes moved down the page, then she turned it over to read the other side. Putting it back, she waited. And waited.

Amanda began to be faintly uneasy. Where was he?

He'd said it shouldn't be long. There must be some problem. Should she go and see for herself? No, she would not, she decided, she'd better wait right here in her room, unless she was told where to move.

She had glanced worriedly at her wristwatch a half-dozen times before he finally returned. He knocked at the door and she opened it to let him in. One glance at his face sent her spirits plummeting. Sharp lines ran down the sides of his mouth and his brows angled in a deep frown.

"No . . ." she began uncertainly.

He was shaking his head. "Completely booked, just like I heard. Can you believe it? Filled up. Everything."

"There's a man across the hall . . ." she offered hopefully.

He nodded dismally. "Two. Truthfully, there's not one space available anywhere on the ship."

There was something about the way he was looking at her that made her wary.

"Oh, there is one possibility," he began cautiously, "one possible solution. They can put you up temporarily. With the nurse in her quarters, until we reach Hawaii."

She distrusted that light flickering in the back of his eyes. He wasn't telling the whole story. "And after we reach Hawaii?" she prodded.

His voice was a shade too smooth. "They are terribly sorry, embarrassed, I would say, about the mix-up. So they will not only refund your entire fare, guarantee you space on the next sailing, when the ship returns, but will fly you home in style." He gave her a reassuring smile, also a little too smooth. "I shouldn't be a bit surprised if they might not do more, maybe a night or two in a luxury hotel in Hawaii before you fly home."

She simply looked at him, not trusting herself at the

moment to utter one single word. Inside she was furious. *She? She was the one expected to give up her trip?*

He was apparently pleased with the arrangement and was clearly expecting her to go along with it, if not cheerfully, then at least grudgingly.

She took a long deep breath and began in a voice that came out too high, too light altogether, "There was, of course, no such possible arrangement that could be made for you instead of me?"

"Oh, no," he said firmly, "quite impossible. It is absolutely necessary for me to make this trip, at this time. It cannot possibly be postponed."

"It is not my fault the mistake was made," she spoke with a show of anger. "I might say that I cannot change my trip, either. It took a long time to arrange for this cruise. It is the only time I can go and ... well, I'm going!" She set her jaw stubbornly and leaned back firmly against the sofa as if she were staking out her claim by the very act.

She saw his face beginning to redden and his lips compress. He looked absolutely inflexible.

"Frankly," she said, "I can see how the mistake was made. *Wynne*. They thought you were a female with that name. So they put us together. Clearly you are the one who was incorrectly booked, so ..." She shrugged.

"Wynne is a man's name, too!" Small sparks of temper flared in his eyes.

"Wynn ... maybe, but with an *e* on the end?" She was being a bit snippy, she told herself, but his smug assumption that she should be quite willing to change all *her* plans made her angry.

"It was my father's name. And my grandfather's," he said icily.

There followed a long stubborn silence. Amanda folded her arms obstinately across her chest, her under-lip protruding the slightest bit. She let her eyes stare everywhere but at the man standing a few feet from her.

Finally he broke the silence. "Well," he said curtly, "for the last time, won't you please be willing to go along with the suggestion of a later trip? Certainly it could be arranged."

"No, it's impossible. I'm lucky to have been able to come now." Amanda knew that was true. If she went back now, Mr. Leland would never give way again.

"Well?" He was curt now. "You won't go?"

She shook her head vigorously.

Again the silence.

This time Amanda spoke. "And you?"

"This is my room. Sorry. I'm staying."

He looked at her for a full moment, then shrugged. "All right, Miss"—he hesitated—"whatever your name is, I'll give you your choice. Which do you want, the upper or lower bunk?"

Chapter 2

Amanda gazed at him blankly. For a few seconds she was not certain she had actually heard what she thought she had. Then her lips tightened in a firm obstinate line. If this was his idea of humor!

"That isn't a terribly amusing remark, Mr. Harrison." Her tone was exceedingly cool.

He shrugged carelessly. "Very well, since you don't seem to care for any suggestion I've made, I'd be delighted to hear anything else you have to offer. Other than my leaving this particular stateroom, this particular trip."

She bit at her lip, hesitating, unsure. What frustrated her was that she really couldn't think of any solution, other than the one he had just refused to consider. He was gazing back at her with an air of unruffled self-command.

"It's a ridiculous idea, absolutely impossible, our sharing the same room," she sputtered.

He took a few steps and sat down at the other end of the sofa, stretching out his legs and leaning back as if the whole thing were simple . . . and settled.

"Why is it impossible?" He couldn't have sounded more casual. The toe of one shoe moved up and down calmly, as if there was no question of a problem.

"It's impossible!" She knew she was repeating herself, but she couldn't think of what else to say.

"Then, my dear young lady, I'm afraid that leaves you without a choice." He glanced at his wristwatch. "The purser will be showing up at our door in about fifteen or twenty minutes. I talked to his assistant, but the purser himself is going to take care of the problem. So I suggest you tell him you will accept the offer to plan your trip for a later date. Because"—now the casual air was replaced with doggedness—"I am staying. Here. In this stateroom."

Outrage swept over her. "I hope you don't consider yourself a gentleman. I certainly don't. Any man with even the smallest amount of courtesy . . ."

He spoke smoothly across her words. "No doubt. All the same, I'm here to stay. That is my choice, my decision. I wouldn't presume to make up your mind for you." There was nothing to ruffle the composure of that voice.

They sat side by side on the sofa, locked in an unyielding silence. She slid a quick look at the strong profile and was immediately irritated at the faint show of satisfaction at the corner of his mouth. How could he be so wretchedly obstinate? She had told him she had to take this trip now. Why couldn't he be a little gracious?

Suddenly he turned his head toward her. "If you are at all worried about—your virtue, so to speak—then I can assure you that you have my word, you will be as safe as if you were with a cousin—no, better make that, with your mother. I'm not without some sympathy, you know, or understanding. If you can't, truly, go at any other time, and I certainly can't, then it seems to me that we can reach only one possible decision." There was a slight twitch to his eyebrows. "Frankly, I'd much prefer to be alone or, if absolutely necessary, with another man to share the room. I think that under the circumstances, I am being very generous."

She made no reply to that condescending remark, but

sat there, doggedly determined not to be edged out of her stateroom assignment. But inside she was seething. *He* was being generous? With something he didn't have the right to?

He glanced again at his watch. "You don't have much time to think it over, the purser is due now any minute. I'm set, but you don't seem to be."

She started to say "but it's impossible" all over again, for the third time, but instead closed her mouth on the words. How could she possibly agree to such an arrangement? She felt a curious reluctance to even think about it.

There was the sound of firm footsteps coming down the hall. They slowed, then halted outside the stateroom. A brief knock and Wynne gave her a knowing nod, then got to his feet to open the door.

A harried-looking ship's officer stepped inside, apologizing profusely. "I'm sorry to be so long in getting down here to talk to you, but you know what it's like for the purser's office shortly after sailing."

Amanda didn't, not really, but one glance at the purser's harassed expression made it clear enough.

The purser was a tall, extremely thin man, of late middle age, with pale-blue eyes that peered at them worriedly through steel-rimmed glasses. He faced them, perspiring a little across the high forehead and rubbing his hands together nervously. "Now"—his voice sounded regretful—"we seem to have a problem with our stateroom, don't we?" He didn't wait for them to reply but continued, "As I understand it, you both were assigned to stateroom 224 and by some regrettable mistake along the line somewhere, it was assumed that"—he gave them a tight little smile—"that you were of the same sex."

"True," Wynne said solemnly, and Amanda wondered if he were trying to be facetious.

"It presents quite a problem, Miss Conklin"—the purser gave a little nod of his head toward her—"as my assistant explained to Mr. Harrison. We are completely booked for the entire cruise, top of the season, you understand? All the staterooms are filled."

Since this seemed to be the purser's problem, Amanda said nothing, waiting for the officer to make a suggestion, which had better not be the one that she leave the ship when they reached the first port. The calm dark-haired man beside her offered no comment either.

"Now, as I understand was explained to Mr. Harrison, there is one possible solution." The purser was speaking half-apprehensively. "And as it seems completely impossible for him to curtail his trip, you might consider . . ."

"No!" The single syllable burst from Amanda violently.

"Ah, no?" The purser seemed perplexed. "I thought Mr. Harrison had intimated you might just possibly . . . ?" He left the sentence unfinished but with a hopeful lift.

"Very well." Wynne took a slow breath, casting a fleeting look at Amanda. "It has been settled, I believe. We shall not bother you any further; we have solved the contretemps to our own satisfaction. I trust," he added, not quite as certainly.

The purser's eyebrows lifted almost to the edge of his thinning hairline. "That's quite—u'mm—surprising. Would you mind telling me how you have resolved it? As I told you, I really am not able to offer any other accommodations, so if that—"

"No, we are perfectly satisfied with the present one. We will continue to occupy this stateroom as has been previously assigned."

"Oh, but"—the purser's face lengthened—"really, sir, I'm afraid that can't be allowed. Ship's policy, you understand. Some ships allow such arrangements; ours does not."

Wynne's voice took on what Amanda knew was a completely false sound of embarrassment. "I'm afraid we have brought you into what is really a little domestic problem. We are," he said smoothly, "married." Amanda felt her nerves recoil in shock. "But," continued Wynne blandly, "we have retained our individual names. My wife"—he gave her a fond glance—"is what you might term a modern woman, a feminist, and wishes to retain her maiden name. Unfortunately, and if you are a married man yourself you will understand, we found ourselves in a feverish domestic argument. No doubt because we were overtired and overwrought by preparations for the trip. And . . . well, it ended in my wife's demanding another stateroom."

Amanda swallowed her anger. He was making her sound like a fool, and what's more, making her an accomplice in an out-and-out deception. She started to speak, then realized that, if she did, there seemed to be only that one other solution. And no trip. For he obviously had convinced the officers that his occupancy was somehow important. Hating herself for her self-indulgence, she remained silent.

The purser stood, hands on hips, a perplexed look on his face. "I really don't . . ." he began, then stopped. He shook his head. "Well, yes, it would be all right in that case. It would not be the first time, I admit, when married people have used their own names, but I must say it is usually in the case of rather famous individuals, who are both actors, for instance, or other people of some renown."

"Oh, I'm sure you will find it increasingly true today, when the wife wishes to retain her own name, that is, her maiden name," Wynne said in a maddeningly agreeable way. Amanda clenched her teeth together and attempted a small tight smile.

The purser backed a step toward the door. "I must be

getting back to the office; there are several pressing matters requiring my attention. If you are certain that the matter has been settled," he said uncomfortably.

"Oh, indeed it has," Wynne cheerfully responded. Then apparently conscious that Amanda had said practically nothing, he turned to her, saying, "It's fine now, isn't it, dear?"

She was startled into speech. "Oh, yes, yes, it is." And despised herself for saying so.

"Then, I'll bid you good evening." The purser looked uncertain whether to be either relieved that the matter had so easily been settled or a little irritated that his time had been taken for what appeared to be a domestic quarrel. A small exasperated sigh escaped from him as he left.

Amanda waited a full thirty seconds after the door closed before bursting out, "I resent that! Lying to the man, saying we are married."

He gave her an impatient look. "My dear young woman, I thought it was so blasted important that you make this trip. Be sensible, he wasn't going to tolerate our presence as two complete strangers, man and woman, occupying the same stateroom. Don't think for a minute that I'm enthralled at the way this has turned out. You have a tongue, you could have called me a liar in front of the purser. You didn't. So stop griping now."

He turned away to yank a suitcase from the floor and place it on the end of the sofa. "Now, which drawers do you want? I'll move my clothes from that closet if you would rather have that particular one."

Her mind was revolving uselessly, this whole thing was so improbable! It couldn't be going to happen. Yet here it was, and here she was.

"I don't mind," she said stiffly. "Take whichever you wish. I—I think I'll go up on deck for a while." She needed to get out of there, away from the situation for a little. How could she pull herself together with this maddening individual pulling out socks and pajamas in the most nonchalant way possible? The whole ridiculous predicament didn't seem to disturb him at all.

She had her hand on the doorknob when he looked up to say cheerfully, "Don't forget to come back in time for us to get to the dining salon on time. We had better put in a few token appearances together, then we can pretty much go our own way and let the situation take care of itself. Say"—he grinned at her—"I know your name is Conklin, but what's your first name? There's only A. L. Conklin on your baggage tags. It does seem to me I'd better have that information in mind."

"Amanda," she said tersely, and went out into the hall, shutting the door quietly but firmly behind her. As she walked away, she was reminded of Graham Moore. She had assured him there was no encumbrance in the way of a husband. What was he going to think now? And she was the confident person who, not very many minutes ago, had firmly decided to not let anything spoil this trip.

She sighed. Nancy, one of the girls at work, had warned her pessimistically that, likely, there'd be no attractive young men on this trip. "Only old, married, retired types," she'd insisted. Amanda wondered what Nancy would think if she knew that there were actually too many. Certainly one too many. Wynne Harrison was attractive-looking, all right, but she most certainly could do without him.

As she passed the lounge, she could hear the sound of music, the tinkle of glasses, and laughter. She had little desire to go in, for right now all she wanted to do was to go out on deck, to be alone so that she could try to wend her way out of the confused tangle in her mind.

Outside, leaning on the rail, she looked out at the night full of stars, conscious of the ocean swashing rhythmically against the side of the ship. The wind blew her hair and the smell of the sea blended with the spiciness of the frangipani lei.

Try as she would, she could not think of any other possible solution to the predicament in which she found herself.

Slowly her resolution hardened. Very well, stay she would. She would remain out of the stateroom all day; after all, she had not come this long way to stay inside a tiny enclosure when the wonderful world of a cruise ship was available. Evenings? Yes, that, too, could be arranged, she decided. There would certainly be enough activity scheduled for those hours. So, if the two of them would each keep scrupulously to themselves, and he clearly had as little interest in her as she had in him, then they would be in the same room for only the period of sleep. If they had been friends, or had any romantic interest in each other, it wouldn't be the same thing at all. This was pure necessity, the sole alternative.

The solution didn't please her, but she grudgingly resigned herself to it.

Several couples strolled out onto the deck, and Amanda was aware that the dinner hour would be soon approaching. Turning reluctantly from the rail, she started back toward her stateroom. Halfway down the passageway, she saw a man coming toward her, one she instantly recognized. Graham Moore. He lifted a hand at her and quickened his step as he approached.

"Hello, again. How about turning around and coming up to the lounge with me for a quick before-dinner drink? Or, if you don't care for one, how about chatting with me while I have one?" His gray eyes smiled down at her.

Oh, dear, now what? "I—I—" she stammered, swallowed, and then said hurriedly, "Not right now, thank you. I—I must change." She gestured weakly at her blue pantsuit. "Travel clothes."

"You look fine to me," he said reluctantly. "But as you wish. I'll see you later?"

It didn't sound like just a polite social gesture; it was a direct question, and he was looking at her expectantly.

What could she do? Stand there in the hall and say, "Well, you see, it's this way, there was a man in my stateroom and he . . . and I . . . ?" No, she couldn't, not here, not now, with people going past them all the time on their way to the lounge or dining room. It was too public. So she did the only thing she could think of at the moment, she gave him a feeble smile and murmured, "I expect so."

It's begun already, she thought glumly. The sort of evasion, the type of petty deception that was bound to go along with this whole stupid situation. Why in the world had she ever agreed to it, except that there was no other way?

When she reached her stateroom, she started to take out her key, thought better of it, and knocked, just in case Wynne was there.

He pulled open the door, stepping aside as she slipped past him into the room.

"I was just about to start to look for you. We ought to be thinking of dinner shortly." His tone was businesslike, and Amanda, for the first time, really, reflected that he probably didn't think this such a great arrangement either. He had said that earlier, but she had been so overwrought by her own stunned reaction that she hadn't given much thought to it. Now he might be speaking to a secretary or a business associate.

She glanced at him curiously. She had no idea what he did for a living. Maybe she ought to know; someone might ask and it would seem a little strange not being able to answer.

He was putting on a tie, peering into the mirror as he looped the knot carefully.

"I suppose I ought to know, since it will be assumed we are married," she said, "what you do for a living."

For a brief second his hands stilled, then he spoke crisply, "I am a writer, I do travel books. That's why I'm on this particular cruise. I've a deadline to meet. After this mix-up, I'm not sure how glowing my report will be."

He reached for his jacket in the closet. "I've unpacked and the steward has taken my empty suitcases. Gives us a little more room, which we can certainly use." He glanced around the small cabin. "I expect you'll want to do the same."

"There won't be time now, but I'll do it after dinner," she said, pulling herself close to the sofa so that he could get by. He was right, they could use more space, for every time they passed each other, they brushed arms.

"Then I'll give you the place to yourself, Amanda," he said diffidently. "I'll meet you at the door of the dining room in"—he glanced at his watch—"twenty minutes. Enough?"

"I'll try," she said as he went out.

As soon as he had left the room, she locked the door and turned to open her suitcase. Carrying a dress into the bathroom, she turned and locked that door, too. She had just time for a quick shower. As she stood under the sharp spray of water, Amanda wondered what she was going to say to Graham. As far as he was concerned, was she or wasn't she married? Oh, damn, she thought, the water spattering down on her bare shoulders, this whole thing has become such a mess.

Toweling quickly after her bath, she dressed, slipping a short-sleeved white knit dress over her head, a touch of color to her lips a red belt, red shoes, and she was ready. She tossed the mane of silky blond hair and gave her reflection in the mirror a rueful smile. This trip was certainly turning out to be anything but uneventful.

Wynne was waiting for her at the door of the dining salon, chatting casually to the headwaiter. As she approached, her pseudo-husband glanced up, and for an instant she caught an unguarded flash in his eyes that was frankly approving of what he saw. Then he stepped forward to join her.

"Ah, Mrs. Harrison, may I show you to your table?" The august gray-haired waiter was beaming majestically at her.

She covered her sudden start with an uneven smile. "Oh, yes, thank you." Mrs. Harrison indeed! She wanted to kick the ankle of that bland-faced, dark-haired man who was touching her elbow, guiding her to a table in an irreproachable husbandly fashion.

As soon as they were seated across from each other at a table for two, and the headwaiter departed, Amanda sputtered under her breath, "You have some nerve. Why do you say we are married to everyone? I thought we had only to satisfy the purser's conscience, not the whole ship's."

His fond smile was clearly for the sake of others who might be looking, his low-pitched voice was not. "Don't be a little dummy! How long do you think it would be before that little bit of news wound up in the purser's ear?" he snapped. "Look, you either decide to go along with this—and I don't enjoy it either—this little theatrical performance, or you don't. Make your choice, but you can't have it both ways. You ought to be able to figure that out."

Before she could frame a reply, a waiter was at their table, smiling and handing them a large shining menu, saying he would return in a moment for their order.

Amanda's state of mind was not improved by the arrival of Graham Moore. He passed their table in the wake of the headwaiter, starting slightly when he saw her. He gave a quick curious look at her table companion, said, "Good evening," and went on by to a table a short distance away.

"Who's that?" Wynne asked casually, picking up a stalk of celery from the relish tray that was already on the table.

"A passenger. Graham Moore. He has the room across the hall," she replied shortly.

Wynne eyed her curiously. "U'mm, too bad, hate to spoil his trip if he has designs on you, but it looks like I must be presumed to have prior claim."

He bit cheerfully into his celery, chewed it a moment, swallowed, and then said, "Sorry, kid. Remember, you can't get too obviously and publicly chummy with any other man. And you shouldn't kick, it doesn't do my romantic hopes any good, either. And there's a stunning-looking redhead across the room."

"If she's the one I saw boarding, I'm doing you a favor," Amanda said tartly.

Wynne grinned across the table. "That's the spirit! Now you are making sounds like I'd expect from a wife, which is maybe why I've never married." Then the grin faded. "Speaking of such things, before we get any further along with this arrangement, I think we should appreciate the danger of propinquity. I really should warn you that I'm not interested in becoming involved in any romantic relationship, with you or with anyone else, at the present time. It's a business trip for me, and I don't want to get mired down with emotional encounters, either of the serious or of the shipboard variety. I'm certain you understand."

"Nor do I have any such interest," she responded frostily. "Unfortunately, and through no fault of our own, we were assigned to the same stateroom. I can see no reason for it to present additional problems." He needn't worry about her showering him with unwelcomed advances, she reflected irritably.

"Good," he said, turning his attention to the menu, pursing his lips thoughtfully over the wide choice offered.

She bent over her own menu, thinking how strange and a bit ridiculous it was that this man could so easily irritate her by nothing more than his basic placid self-confidence. He was so supremely sure of himself.

After the entrée had been consumed and their plates carried away, Wynne looked up over the top of the menu. "Now, for dessert. How about *baba au rhum*, guaranteed only nineteen hundred calories a bite?" His eyes turned back to the page. "Or maybe chocolate cake with Swiss fudge icing? A slim young thing like you ought to indulge while there is time and waistline to spare."

She shook her head. "Only coffee, please. This is the very first meal on board, the first day. If I should weaken today, then I would again tomorrow and ... until I had no waistline at all." She gave him a small smile. He could be pleasant enough in between those abrasive little flashes of serene self-possession, Amanda realized. In spite of herself and her intention of remaining absolutely detached and aloof, she found herself growing interested as he began telling her about some of the islands they were going to visit. As the waiter put her cup of coffee in front of her and gave the *baba au rhum* to Wynne, she listened to the man across from her.

He nodded toward her coffee. "You'll give that drink up for life, once you taste the specialty of Fiji. *Yaqona*, or *kava*, it's a popular custom as well as a beverage on the island."

She tilted her tawny gold cap of hair. "And what is ... whatever you called it?"

A light flickered amusedly in the depths of the blue eyes. "Wait. I don't want to spoil it for you. You know how it is when someone oversells something and it turns out to be less than you expected?" He hunched a shoulder. "And don't let anyone tell you it isn't a fascinating drink. An acquired taste, of course, but worth the try."

Wynne attacked the *baba au rhum* with enthusiasm. Finally he leaned back to smile at her. "You're making a mistake taking only coffee. That was some dessert. Are you in training to become a Spartan?"

"Not at all."

"Then, shall we go? By the way, tonight's seating is only temporary. From now on we'll be seated at a table for six. Or so that regal being, the headwaiter, informs me."

"Won't that be . . . difficult?" she asked uncertainly.

"You mean questions? We're bound to get them anyhow while we are on board. Frankly I think it's not such a bad idea. Under the circumstances, we may find our situation can be trying enough without having to face each other, and only each other, over every meal."

He certainly made it clear, she thought, they weren't to inflict themselves on each other any more than necessary. Well, that was fine with her.

Rising, he moved around to pull out her chair, and they left the dining room together. As they went through the foyer, he asked, "Are you planning to return to the room now?"

She shook her head. "Not right away. I've never been on a sea voyage before and I want to be out on deck as much as I can."

"Then, if you don't mind, I've some paperwork to take care of. Come back anytime and I'll vacate the room for you. Until time to turn in," he said blandly.

"All right," she said jerkily, trying to shove that last phrase of his from her mind, it made her uncomfortable.

He left, and Amanda pushed through the heavy doors to go out on deck. A rush of sea air met her, touching her lips with the taste of salt spray. She circled around the deck, watching the smooth pattern of the moon splaying out over the water.

Finally she chose a deck chair, leaning back in it, fascinated by the closeness of the stars, the clarity of the night. Before long, the rhythmic wash of the sea against the side of the ship, the freshness of the air, lulled her gently and she found her eyelids growing heavy and languid.

"I've been looking for you." The words jerked her abruptly from her somnolent state. Her eyes flying open, she saw Graham Moore standing in front of her, gazing down. "Mind if I sit by you?"

"Not at all, please do," she said automatically, then recoiled a little within herself. This could get sticky. She reminded herself that she hadn't yet planned how to explain Wynne, especially when she had so positively stated she had no husband. Would it be better to try to be frank about it, or simply allow him to presume she had been a liar about claiming her single status? She couldn't decide, so she said nothing, remembering Wynne's warning about word getting back to the purser. So, chiding herself for her indecision, she evaded the issue for the moment.

And, of course, she was confronted with the issue right away. "I see I was a little slow in trying to date you up for tonight. I told you how stiff the competition is and I forgot to take my own advice. Well, how about a swim tomorrow morning?"

That ought to be safe enough, certainly. After all, even married people, genuinely married people, don't isolate themselves from other people, surely. So she said, "Fine, I'd love it."

For a while they talked, Amanda cautiously skirting

dangerous subjects as one steps gingerly through a mine field. He was knowledgeable about art and travel, and spoke of Gauguin and the man's strange life in Tahiti. She lay back in her chair, listening, until she abruptly realized it was growing late.

She sat erect, fumbling by her side for her purse. "I really must be going down to my stateroom. I still have to unpack. I'll see you tomorrow by the pool." That last was a bit of weasling, but she didn't want him knocking on her door, not yet, not until she had come to her decision.

She wasn't quick enough in taking her leave, for he was already on his feet. "I'll walk back with you."

She swallowed uncomfortably. This would not do at all. But there was no way she could think of to discourage him without sounding terribly rude. She should tell him, she prodded herself, she should tell him! And could not quite bring herself to. Tonight she would decide what to say and how to say it, and tomorrow . . . tomorrow for sure!

They went down the hall, and as they approached the vicinity of her stateroom, she searched frantically through her mind for a way to get him to leave before she had to knock and Wynne come to the door. Or should she unlock it, slip in, and maybe find Wynne in an unexpected stage of undress? Either way was difficult. And a problem.

They were almost in front of 224 when Graham asked idly, "Oh, by the way, did your roommate arrive?"

She almost missed her step. "Oh, ah, well, yes," she said, not turning her head lest he catch the expression on her face.

At her door she murmured, "Good night, Graham. See you in the morning," and busied herself over her purse as if searching for her key, waiting for him to leave.

But he stood there, smiling at her. Amanda hesitated,

not wanting to knock, not wanting to unlock the door, pushed for an immediate choice and unable to stall any longer.

"May I unlock it for you?" he asked as she drew out her key.

"Oh, no, thanks," she said, slipping the key in quickly, ready to slide inside rapidly before he got a glimpse of Wynne.

But the doorknob was jerked out of her hand and Wynne stood in the open doorway.

"Oh, sorry, Amanda. I meant to get back up on deck and join you." He bobbed his head at Graham. "Good evening."

Amanda was frozen to the spot, conscious of Graham's eyes upon her back.

Chapter 3

There was a momentary silence, then Graham replied, "Good evening," his voice curt. She heard him take a step to open his own door, but she did not look back at him. She felt stupid and humiliated. Though Wynne had warned her about telling anyone, she would certainly have to make an exception for Graham, she knew now, and she had been incredibly foolish not to have made the decision sooner. Why had she allowed herself to be irresolute?

And Wynne? He was completely untroubled. He held the door open as Amanda stepped inside, then closed it behind her. She opened her mouth once or twice to say something, then didn't. Why did he have to open the door with that calm proprietary air? Yet, underneath, she realized she was mentally lashing out at him simply because she had appeared so deceitful in front of Graham.

The beds were made up and Wynne was gathering up some of his papers. "I'll take a few turns around the deck while you unpack, if that's what you plan to do. I'll be back in about an hour?"

"Yes. All right," she said tersely.

Before leaving, he gave Amanda a quizzical look. Jerking his head toward the door, he asked, "That guy going to be a problem for you?"

She turned her head quickly to look at him. "Why? Why do you ask?"

He shrugged. "Oh, he looked miffed, surprised, all that sort of thing. I presume I was rather unexpected."

Amanda began unlocking her suitcases, her hands busy, her face hidden because her back was to him. "You were. I'm going to have to explain to him. You see, I told him earlier that I wasn't married."

"Okay, if you think you must. Let's hope he keeps it to himself. Frankly, it isn't that I think the purser cares one way or the other, but he's got to go through the motions, I guess."

She twisted her head to look at him. "Don't worry, Graham's no problem."

He was, though, in a way, she thought. Graham was fun, certainly extremely attractive, the type any sensible girl would be delighted to encounter on a cruise, or anywhere else. Now it was spoiled somewhat, all because of the mistake in room assignment, that and that stubborn man stuffing his key into his coat pocket, whistling softly through his teeth. She wished she could believe it was that vitally important for him to be making this particular trip, that he couldn't somehow have postponed it until later.

"See you in about an hour," he said, "I'll take the top bunk." And was gone.

Amanda unpacked mechanically, her hands carefully unfolding clothes, shaking them out, hanging them in her closet, putting smaller things in drawers. Carrying some of her cosmetics into the small bathroom, she opened the door of the medicine cabinet. There, scrupulously consigned to two of the narrow shelves, were *his* things: shaving lotion, toothbrush, a small black comb, toothpaste. She hesitated, holding her own toothbrush uncertainly. It gave her a most peculiar feeling, to be sharing this space with a man, a stranger at that. There was an odd indication of something so dreadfully intimate, somehow, in placing her things beside his.

She firmed her chin. She was being a little silly, wasn't she? After all, she reflected ironically, she was sharing a bedroom with him, why should she hesitate in sharing a medicine cabinet?

When the room steward had removed her empty luggage, she sank down on the edge of the lower bed. What she really ought to do was change into her nightgown and crawl into bed, pretending to be asleep by the time he returned. But she sat there, an uncomfortable tightening of nerves gripping the back of her neck. There was no evading the thought that tonight she would be sleeping a few feet away from an attractive, if irritating man whom she hadn't seen or known until a few hours ago. The moments slipped by unheeded.

She roused herself to her feet. Best she undress and slip into bed without delay, lest he return unexpectedly. That thought spurred her into feverish activity now. How long had she been sitting there? She had no notion, so she rushed into the bathroom, locking the door firmly, then slipped out of her clothes and into her nightgown, shoving her hands through her dressing robe.

She hesitated before opening the door, then bent to listen, pressing her ear close to the wood. There was no sound in the other room. Unlocking the door, she pulled it open a crack and peered out. The room was empty. Quickly she slipped out of the bathroom and, yanking back the covers, rapidly squirmed into bed. Wriggling out of her robe, laying it carefully within reach at the foot of her bed, she lay back on her pillow, her heart pulsing faster than usual. Reaching up, she flipped off her bed light, the only remaining glow in the room came from the small one on the wall above his bed.

Don't *pretend* to go to sleep, relax and *go to sleep*, she instructed herself firmly. She didn't, of course, but lay stiffly in bed, her ears nervously attuned to his return. At last she heard footsteps outside, a faint knock she pretended not to hear, a moment's hesitation, and then the soft click of a key in the lock. A shaft of light from the hallway speared across the room, then muted dusk was back as the door shut. She lay very still, making an effort to breathe slowly and deeply as if asleep, her eyes shut tightly.

He tiptoed into the bathroom after fumbling in a drawer. Shutting the door behind him, he locked it firmly. Her lips tightened. Surely he didn't expect her to break in on him!

Finally the door opened, again came the furtive footsteps, crossing the floor, mounting the small ladder up to the top bunk. There was the soft crush of mattress, then the light clicked off, leaving the room in complete darkness. Amanda opened her eyes, listening to the sound of a quickly silenced yawn above her, the rustling sound of someone settling down, then silence.

Amanda tried to turn her mind off, to forget about Wynne and go to sleep, but for a long time she lay staring into the darkness until at long last her eyes flickered several times, then shut, and she drifted off.

A faint sound reached into her dreams, stirring her into the half-world that is part sleep and part wakefulness. She nuzzled her head deep into her pillow, as if to escape from the rhythmic buzzing that annoyed her ears. Her eyes blinked once or twice, then flew open wide, and she sat up in bed abruptly, her gaze riveted on the bathroom door. The sound of an electric razor came from within. She gave a hurried glance at her watch. It was morning. She sat there for a dazed second or two, the covers pulled up to her neck, all the events of yesterday rushing back.

The hum of the razor stopped. Silence, then the bathroom door opened and he came out, clad in gray slacks and blue sport shirt. Amanda lay back against the pillow, the covers up to her chin as she peered over the top.

"Oh, you're awake. Good morning." He was imperturbable. They might have been casually encountering in the park or at a supermarket. "Hope I didn't awaken you."

"No, no, you didn't," she said untruthfully, clutching the blanket in tense fingers.

He turned toward the closet and hauled out a sweater, pulling it over his head, then gave her a polite unconcerned smile. "I think I'll go up on deck, they're serving coffee beside the pool. If you want to join me, fine; if not, I'll probably see you later somewhere about. I don't think we have to inflict ourselves on each other any more than necessary, or let it spoil any of our plans, as long as we are circumspect." His nod of the head was like a courteous tip of the hat as he sauntered out, shutting the door behind him.

He hadn't given her a chance to make a reply of any kind, she thought indignantly, struggling to a sitting position once again. Inflict themselves on each other! She glared at the tie he'd left hanging on the closet door. What was that remark supposed to mean, she wondered, her cheeks hot. Did he think she would presume on their situation?

Shoving the covers back, grabbing her robe, and elbowing into it, she padded toward the bathroom. She scowled at her reflection in the mirror, conscious of the scent of his shaving lotion pervading the room. Men! Men! She picked up a washcloth and scrubbed at her face hard with cold water, wondering why Fate had played such a dirty trick on her on this trip. Maybe, she reflected, I don't mean Men! I mean Man! That Wynne Harrison irritated her all out of proportion! Graham ... at the thought of him, she had a quick sinking feeling inside. This morning she must explain and the thought wasn't terribly inviting.

But armed with a firm resolve to do just that, she dressed carefully, slipping into white slacks and a coral jersey, a coral ribbon catching up her blond hair. Leaning close to the mirror, she touched her lips with a coordinated shade of coral lipstick.

The sun was brilliant, almost blinding, as she stepped out on deck. Passengers were everywhere: in deck chairs, leaning against the railing, taking pictures of each other, or simply strolling about, eyeing everyone else with interested curiosity. Amanda made her way up to the pool terrace and stood for a moment looking about her. Sitting in a lounge chair, some distance away, was Wynne, his long legs stretched out in front of him indolently, a cup of coffee on the table at one side. And on the other side, long mascaraed lashes sweeping up at him, sat the red-haired girl whom she had noticed yesterday. Amanda was close enough to see those lashes and, for that matter, a good deal of the girl herself. She voluptuously filled a brief orange bikini, bright against her golden tan skin, and she was leaning toward Wynne intimately, red-tipped nails touching his arm as she tilted her head at him. They were chatting like old friends, and for a moment Amanda felt oddly left out. She frowned at herself for that momentary silly reaction, then turned away to stroll to the other side to find an empty chair and sink into it.

She deliberately turned her eyes and thoughts away from the pair on the far side of the terrace. A few moments later, she rose to get a cup of coffee and had barely returned with it when Graham appeared, coming up the steps, immaculate in white slacks and a short-sleeved jersey.

He saw her, stopped uncertainly, then strolled in her

direction. He did not sit, but stood stiffly in front of her, as if not quite certain how to open the conversation.

"Good morning, Graham. I think I owe you an explanation," Amanda blurted out. "I mean, I didn't intend to say anything that wasn't so, it's just not what you think ..." The conversation appeared to get away from her, and she halted, looking up at him apologetically.

He sat down on the edge of the chair next to her, almost defensively, his gray eyes polite but cool.

"It's quite all right," he said stonily. "Perhaps I misunderstood you."

"I'm not married," she said nervously, "not really." Then she realized she was making matters worse and that only made things look even more appalling. She rushed to explain. "It's just that this man, Wynne Harrison, and I—well, we have the same room because there was a mix-up," she said fumblingly, a hint of excuse creeping into her voice, feebly, infuriatingly.

Abruptly she halted. "Oh, darn! It's all so stupid, I feel like a fool explaining such a weird situation." Gathering her wits together, she told him, speaking quickly, her defensiveness gone. Either he would understand or he wouldn't, and if he wouldn't, it couldn't be helped, she realized.

He did. In a way. But he slanted an odd look at her. "You must admit that it isn't the usual method of travel, except in liberated circles. The meaningful-relationship sort of thing. For a moment you had me confused." Then, suddenly, he grinned, his white teeth flashing amusedly. "You don't suppose that this Wynne person would be willing to trade roommates with me? Mine seems to be a stodgy character, addicted to stale cigars and girlie magazines."

She laughed, relieved at his acceptance of the situation. "It could be worse, I suppose. I might have gotten your roommate. And I hate cigars!"

"Or you could have drawn me." The gray eyes held hers. "But I'm afraid I couldn't have promised to be so scrupulously detached as you say this Wynne Harrison is."

"Oh, he is," she assured him. "But, Graham, I'd rather the truth about our arrangement doesn't get around, in case the purser would feel it necessary to take a stand." Suddenly she giggled, her eyes crinkling. "You know, this is so insane that I can't even begin to cope with it, emotionally or mentally. It's like a drawing-room comedy carried to absurd proportions. I never dreamed anything like this could occur, least of all to me."

Graham turned his head momentarily to look at Wynne and the red-haired girl. Amanda glanced over the same way. She felt the least bit irritated at the elaborate attention Wynne was displaying toward his new friend. And he had given *her* that pious little lecture about being circumspect! His profile was turned so that she could see he was laughing, obviously enjoying the company.

The girl had handed Wynne a tube of what appeared to be suntan lotion, for he looked at it a moment, hesitated, then started studiously applying it to her shoulders, while she was looking flirtatiously into his face.

Amanda sat back, lifting her coffee cup, and devoted herself to drinking the last of the golden fluid, stone cold by now. Graham had returned his attention to her. "The arrangement doesn't seem to hamper him," he said dryly.

"Well, if there are any repercussions, I am not going to be the one to get out of 224," Amanda stated positively.

"Does he have to make the trip? I should think he'd have been willing to give way to you." Graham pulled a cigarette package from the pocket of his shirt, offering it to her.

Amanda shook her head, adding, no, it wouldn't bother her at all if he smoked. "I tried to get him to go," she said.

"And . . . ?"

"He said, 'no way' or words to that effect."

"Because of business, I suppose," Graham pursued idly, the blue smoke drifting upward, for an instant masking his eyes. "What does he do, did he say?"

"Travel writer, he does books or magazine articles, I forget which. Anyhow, he claims he has a deadline and can't put off the trip."

Graham appeared to abandon the subject. Squinting up at the warm sun overhead, he said, "How about a quick swim? Then we can grab a quick breakfast from the buffet table up here."

The idea appealed to Amanda. Pushing herself up from the deck chair, she said, "Good. I'll go down and change. Meet me here?"

He stubbed out the cigarette in a metal ashtray on the table and stood up. "I'll go down and change, too." Then he glanced over at the back of Wynne's head, studiously attentive to the girl beside him, but made no comment other than to answer her question. "Meet here then, in about fifteen minutes?"

She nodded and they began walking toward the steps that would take them below to the staterooms, casually avoiding the route that would carry them past Wynne and his friend.

If Graham thought anything about her maneuver, he made no mention of it; they chatted of other things as they descended to the lower hallway.

Outside her stateroom, he reached for her hand. "See you in a few minutes, then, Amanda. You know, I'd say this is a budding romance struggling under the most unusual handicap." A quick squeeze of her fingers, and he let himself into his room.

Amanda found the beds made up and the place in order as she entered. Catching a glimpse of her face in the mirror, she saw that it was flushed. Well, Graham certainly believed in moving things right along, she reflected, half amused, half not sure. Granted, it was flattering, she had the faintly uneasy feeling he was a bit too intent. Now, why did I think *intent*, she wondered, I meant ... intense. She paused, staring unseeingly into the mirror. Then she shrugged the thought away and kicked off her slippers. Pulling open one of the dresser drawers, she picked up her bathing suit from it, then padded shoeless toward the bathroom.

She stripped off the white slacks and coral jersey top, only to turn and glance in dismay at her two-piece bathing suit draped on a small stool by her side. Two piece? There was one piece! The bottom part was there, the bra was not. Had she dropped it? Cautiously she opened the door and peered out. There it was, lying right below the drawer where it had fallen. She hesitated a moment. Did she dare dash out quickly in her panties and bra to grab it? Surely the steward was through with the room, and he wouldn't enter, anyhow, without knocking first. And Wynne was safely enthralled with his redhead. Get dressed again in order to rush out a half-dozen steps? Nonsense.

She moved quickly ... but not quickly enough. She had no more than bent to retrieve her bathing suit top when the door clicked and was opened, a startled-faced Wynne stood there. She flung around, raced for the bathroom, slamming the door behind her, locking it, her heart pounding wildly, her anger boiling up in her like a volcano.

"For God's sake, I'm sorry, I apologize!" came Wynne's voice. "I forgot, honest! I had something else on my mind and I forgot. Besides, I saw you and that guy across the hall up on deck, then you disappeared together and I just figured . . ."

"Get out, will you please? Leave the room." Her voice came through the door icily, but the ice did not reach inside her, she was hot with anger and chagrin. He had caught her half-clad and he was standing on the other side of the bathroom door, making excuses. "Go!"

"Want me to hand you"—there was a short pause—"this excuse for part of a bathing suit?" he asked, and she could swear there was a trace of amusement in his tone. It only served to further infuriate her.

"I do not!"

"Okay, I'll hang it on the doorknob of the bathroom. I'm leaving, but . . . I'm sorry, Amanda. It wasn't intentional, I can assure you."

She heard the outer door shut, but she waited a full minute before cautiously unlocking her door, edging it open. There, dangling ridiculously on the knob, was the rest of her pale-green suit. Her hand trembled as she reached to bring it inside before shutting the door once again. Then, grudgingly, she had to admit to herself that he could have been telling the truth. Still, prickles of embarrassment continued to run along under her skin.

Pulling her soft short terry robe over her suit, she left the stateroom and went up to join Graham, who waited by the edge of the pool, broad-shouldered and slim-waisted, in brief striped trunks. Amanda was aware that the tanned young man smiling at her was the eye target of every woman seated about the pool terrace and, she imagined, the envy of those men who were already running to too much waistline and too little hair.

Slipping out of her terry-cloth robe, Amanda was conscious Graham was looking at her. "I don't dare whistle," he said apologetically over a smile, "it would disrupt your carefully erected fake marriage act . . . but I'd like to."

She made a face at him and slipped into the cool
waters of the pool. In seconds, Graham was beside her,
the drops of water beading on his square shoulders.

For the next half-hour they swam and sunned until
Amanda began to feel the stirrings of hunger and said
so. "I suppose it's the sea air, but I'm starved. I think I'll
run below and change."

"Breakfast up here on the terrace with me?"

She hesitated. "Maybe not this time. After all, I have
to maintain the illusion of a young matron to some
degree."

"Hi, there, Moore," a thick voice broke in, and
Amanda raised her head to see a square swarthy face,
harshly lined, with small shrewd eyes fixed on her. He
was short, clad in a bright Hawaiian shirt and belted
slacks that barely restrained a growing paunch. Not an
attractive individual, she decided, then she noticed the
cigar clutched in his hand.

"Hello, Shields," Graham said reluctantly.

The man did not move away, but stood waiting for an
introduction, his cigar now lifted to his mouth by the
stubby fingers that bore two large square-stoned rings.

Graham capitulated politely if not enthusiastically.
"This is Mrs."—he hesitated, not certain how to put it.

"I'm Amanda Conklin." She spoke into his broken sentence.

"Pleased," the man said over the top of his cigar. "I'm
Harry Shields." He kept looking at her with those small
sly eyes, making Amanda's skin crawl in spite of herself.
What a dreadful man. To think that Graham had to put
up with this! She had known immediately who he was.
In comparison, Wynne seemed almost acceptable.

She hurriedly excused herself, saying she must go below to get ready for breakfast, and left, uncomfortably
aware that she was followed by Harry Shields' eyes.

As she approached her stateroom, she paused to dig in

her purse for her key, then stopped. That was what Wynne had done, reached out with his key to unlock the door instinctively, unconsciously, not remembering to knock. She let the key drop back into the bag and lifted her hand to tap twice, lightly.

The door clicked open and Wynne stood there. "I've come down to change for breakfast," she announced stiffly.

He stepped aside to allow her to enter. She waited, but he simply stood there, making no move to leave. She glanced back at him over her shoulder, speaking coolly, "Well . . . ?"

He put his hands on his hips and sighed elaborately. "I suppose that means you'd like me to step outside." There was an amused twitch to his mouth that made her face prickle.

"If you don't mind, though I presume I could carry all my clothes into the bathroom and dress there."

"Okay, I'll get out, but next time you choose the bathroom for dressing, try to take all your clothes," he teased her, an amused glint in his eye.

"Oh, very funny!" She waited until he left the room, tossing her a waggish grin as he did so.

If she were a child, she would have stamped her foot. He was the most infuriating of men! She reached out and locked the door with a snap. She could not erase the memory of his standing there watching, probably with amusement, when she had made her frantic dash for the bathroom, clad only in her scanty underwear.

When she had dressed, she headed for the dining room, where she was greeted by the headwaiter with recognition, "Ah, good morning, Mrs. Harrison, lovely day. Mr. Harrison is already seated at your permanent table. This way, please." Giving her a faint bow, he sailed ahead with imposing dignity while she trailed behind him.

Wynne was sitting at a table with a group of other people and rose to his feet as she approached, clearly in the role of the devoted husband. "Good morning, my dear," he said infuriatingly, giving her a benevolent smile.

She slipped hurriedly into her chair, conscious of a blur of faces at the table around her. Wynne was saying in an apologetic voice, "I'm afraid I don't know all your names yet, but this is my ... wife, Amanda Conklin," he said blandly.

"Conklin? I thought it was Harrison." Amanda followed the voice to its source. She was an immensely fat woman, her huge bosom straining the pink, flowered jersey material of her blouse. She had an unhappy unfriendly face, with a small petulant mouth that drooped at the corners, watery blue eyes that flicked constantly as if in search of some errant prey. With her pulled-back, thin white hair and colorless eyebrows and lashes, she looked like a giant pink frog, Amanda suddenly thought irreverently.

"It is Conklin," Amanda said. "I have retained my maiden name." That was as far as she could go in this deception.

Before the plump woman could make the disapproving comment that was so clearly on her lips, a square-faced, rawboned girl sitting next to Amanda broke into the conversation in a cheery voice. "Oh, I say, have you now? How trendy of you! Wish I had the nerve." Then her ruddy cheeked face sobered. "Wish I had the chance."

Her smile reappeared as she said, "I'm Joan Blakey, from a small town outside of Sydney, Australia."

Amanda had turned to her with a certain amount of relief, glad to have escaped the scathing eye of the other woman. But she didn't entirely manage, for the stentorian voice followed.

"For your information, I am *Mrs.* Hildebrand. And this is my husband, Claude Hildebrand."

Amanda swung her eyes back to see a meek, balding man send her a tentative nervous smile before returning his attention to the plate before him.

Amanda spoke politely to all of them, acknowledging the introductions, then busied herself with unfolding her napkin and taking a sip of water from the glass in front of her. She felt like an utter, utter fool.

Before there was any more conversation from anyone, a lilting voice in back of her said, "Oh, how delightful! I didn't know we'd meet again, Wynne, not so soon, anyhow."

Amanda could almost have guessed. The stunning redhead had slipped into the chair next to Wynne and was turning her not inconsiderable charm on him.

"Oh, hello, Dianne," he said, only the faint reddening of his ear tips showing any sign of his being disconcerted, if indeed he was at all, Amanda decided.

"This is Miss Sayers, Dianne Sayers," he was saying glibly. "I hope I have all your names right. Mrs. Hildebrand, Mr. Hildebrand, Miss Joan Blakey, and this is . . ."

"Don't tell me, I can guess!" Heavily mascaraed eyelashes lifted toward Amanda. "You are Amanda, Amanda Conklin, aren't you? I'm fascinated, I really am. You're the first women's libber I ever met, if you'll excuse my saying so. It's so—so sort of strange, I suppose I'm impossibly behind the times."

"Not at all! I'm with you! I just don't understand these modern girls with these newfangled things! Monkeying with the Bible, I call it," Mrs. Hildebrand said accusingly.

"Now, now, Gertrude," protested Mr. Hildebrand's timid voice, then he quickly subsided at his wife's glare.

Amanda wasn't quite certain whether to giggle or be

indignant. This was all so absurd. She slid a quick glance at Wynne and saw he had the grace, at least, to look embarrassed, but he merely said, "The arrangement, I might say, does suit Amanda and me."

Thankfully the conversation took a less-trying turn as Joan Blakey stepped in with suggestions of things they might wish to see during their stay in her homeland. She spoke of the beauties of the countryside, and the discomfort Amanda had experienced began to ebb away as she listened with genuine interest as the girl's crisply accented voice described the outback country with its sheep stations and told them that what is commonly called a koala bear is not a bear, but a marsupial, with a pouch like a kangaroo.

As they left the table, Joan sidled close to Amanda to say in a low confidential voice, "Don't you mind what that Mrs. Hildebrand says. She's an old wowser, that one is!"

Amanda smiled. "I won't let it bother me." Especially since it doesn't really apply, she thought. Still, it was hard not to squirm inwardly at the look Mrs. Hildebrand had tossed over her shoulder when leaving the dining room.

Wynne caught up with her. "Still annoyed with me? I apologized, you know, about bursting in on you."

He had, of course; so she made no retort, contenting herself with a nod.

"By the way," he went on cheerfully, "you'll find we are married in our ultra-modern way not only in the eyes of the purser, but on the list of the ship's passengers. I forgot to tell you, they came around to see how we wished to be listed."

He shrugged at her sudden look at him. "Not just us, they inquire of everyone. I simply solved the matter by saying you used your maiden name with an Ms. in front of it. It satisfied them, and every advocate of women's liberation will no doubt be around to shake your hand."

"Beginning with Mrs. Hildebrand," she said bitterly. "But I do think you might have consulted me, just out of courtesy, to see how I felt about it. I'm not crazy about Ms."

"You weren't around. Besides, it would reflect on my masculine self-esteem and pride if I had to say, 'Sorry, I've got to ask her first.' It's enough of a put-down to have my spurious wife called by her own name. Personally, I'd never permit it. Never would."

"I'm sure you wouldn't," she replied in a tone that lifted his eyebrows.

They parted, Wynne sauntering off to play a game of shuffleboard, Amanda to the stateroom to get her address book so she could write some notes to friends. On her way back up to the writing room just off the passengers' lounge, she passed down the long hall. Suddenly she was aware of the acrid smell of a cigar. Mr. Shields appeared from one of the bisecting hallways, nearly bumping into her.

He pulled the cigar from his mouth to gaze at her, his hard eyes opening and closing almost automatically—just like a lizard's, she thought abruptly and felt a little shudder of distaste ripple through her.

"We meet again, Miss Conklin, don't we?" he said smoothly.

She responded with a tight smile that did not reach her eyes, as she edged past him and went on down the hall, walking a little faster to put distance between her and the smell of the stale cigar and the encounter with Harry Shields. He's dreadful, he really is, she thought.

Chapter 4

As Amanda leaned over the ship's rail, her eyes searched the horizon for the first green rise of land that would herald the islands of Hawaii and the port of Honolulu. Beside her stood Wynne, a pair of binoculars in his hand.

"I think there's something over there on the left." He lifted the glasses and peered silently for a moment, then turned toward her. "Want to have a look?"

"No, thank you," she answered, not taking her eyes away from the sweep of the ocean ahead.

She heard him draw in an exasperated breath. "Look, Miss Purity, I'm sure there would be nothing compromising in using my binoculars. I'm quite aware that for the past four days you have been scrupulously, almost to the point of extremity, careful to observe propriety where the two of us are concerned. Just because we are unfortunate enough to have to occupy the same stateroom. Don't worry, I'm not going to assault you."

Amanda turned green eyes at him. She wasn't quite sure herself why she felt so rigid in manner around him. "I think that it is difficult enough for us, sharing the same room, meeting at meals, carrying on careful small talk for the benefit of others. I find it trying, I'm certain you do. It seems to me that it is best to maintain an attitude of impersonal distant relationship when we are alone. In fact, I think you yourself suggested that, more or less, at the beginning. And, no, thank you, I really don't wish to use your binoculars."

He leaned on his elbow, facing her, and though her gaze was fixed straight ahead, she was aware of his attention. "Look, Amanda, ever since that first morning when you were changing for a swim, you've been extremely formal and haughty. It was a mistake, I apologized, so why are you so damned stiff-necked? I must say that, as a roommate, it's hardly better than being in with a porcupine."

"Have I ever, in public, acted other than courteously, or wifelike, if you will?" she asked quietly, not meeting his gaze.

"In public, no," he admitted grudgingly. "And what have you ever had to kick about, where my actions are concerned, after that one silly mistake? Anything?"

"Nothing," she replied. "It does seem to me that we agreed that this is the best way to conduct ourselves in the circumstances we are in, that of unwilling roommates."

He didn't answer, and for a moment she was tempted to turn to see what expression was on his face, for she was almost conscious of wheels turning in his mind.

Suddenly he spoke, "I hope you don't blame me for the Hildebrands' asking to have their table changed. I think it's a great improvement without them."

"No, I don't blame you, though I must say I don't relish the idea of anyone's thinking I'm some kind of scarlet woman."

"Well, that young couple, the Babcocks, they're okay. Glad they're replacing that old battle-ax and her poor mouse of a husband."

Suddenly there was a sly teasing in his voice. "I bet I know what's bothering you. You think I'm spending too much time with Dianne, the luscious redhead. Like last night. There was some pretty spectacular moonlight out on deck. I didn't dare ask you to take a walk with me. I was afraid to. She asked me. Is that what's bothering you?"

She knew he was needling her, but it snapped her head around, eyes blazing. "That most certainly isn't it," she flared hotly. "I couldn't care less. I think you deserve each other."

He grinned at her. "Oh, the kitten has claws!" Then the amusement in his face vanished. "Seriously, I just said that to see if I could get a rise out of you. Quite honestly, it's a bit trying to be in constant relationship with the original snow maiden. I'm not suggesting anything but a more-relaxed attitude toward each other. Nothing else at all. You can even go on seeing your boyfriend, Graham, from time to time . . . discreetly."

"Discreetly? You should talk . . ." she began indignantly.

"Ah, ah! It is always with immense circumspection, I assure you. My conduct with the young lady is above criticism." His tone was mocking.

Why did she continue to react so hotly, she wondered? He was the one who had first laid out the rules of conduct, underlining his fear of being involved emotionally. She was merely being careful to observe the agreement. She tried to be cool, to remain aloof, but he seemed to take delight in rousing her temper. Well, she needn't respond. She returned to her search of the horizon, refusing to allow herself to be drawn into a conversation that was so clearly counterproductive.

He spoke again. "Sometimes you act as if you really don't trust me. You can, you know. Completely. I don't mean to be in any way insulting or uncomplimentary, but you aren't exactly the type of girl I'd choose to pursue for any sort of romantic interest. I don't mean that you aren't an attractive person; you are, very much so. What I'm driving at is that you are . . ." He paused, then shrugged his shoulders. "Well, let's just say you can feel completely unthreatened by me. But"—he cocked a quizzical eyebrow at her—"maybe not by that Graham guy."

His tone and his words had brought the blood to her face. The nerve of him, airily placing her in a well-defined pigeonhole. Friendly, but not too friendly for his comfort. As if subtly warning her off of any hope of conquest.

She moistened her lips to hide the sign of their angry trembling, lest he think he'd gotten a rise from her, as she forced herself to calmly meet the gaze of those mocking blue eyes screened by ridiculously thick black lashes. "Irish eyes, put in with a sooty finger," her grandmother once said. The thought flicked through her mind ridiculously, but she managed to reply with an almost condescending air, "I really wouldn't want you to worry, either. If ever I had any emotional reaction to you, which I assure you I had not, then these five days of sharing the same stateroom would have destroyed them."

She gave him an ultra-sweet smile. "You snore, you know."

"I *do not!*" Sparks flashed angrily in the blue eyes.

She contented herself with a prim lifting of her eyebrows. He didn't, of course, but she couldn't resist turning the needle back upon him.

"Can you see Honolulu yet?" a silky voice interrupted them. Amanda turned to see Dianne sauntering up to the railing beside them.

"Just a faint show of land in the distance," Wynne said, and Amanda was aware of a certain amount of relief in his voice. He clearly didn't enjoy being on the receiving end of their interplay of sly digs.

"I do hope you don't mind that I kept Wynne out so late last night," Dianne said in a voice all honey. "He was telling me about the stars. We have a common interest in . . ." She paused for a second then added, "Astronomy. Please don't misunderstand, it's all perfectly innocent. Isn't it, Wynne?" The girl laid her hand intimately on his arm, smiling up at him.

"Oh, he's perfectly trustworthy, he says so himself," Amanda couldn't resist saying placidly. That girl was impossible, she thought. What if Wynne were really her husband and she loved him? Why, this little red-haired vixen was trying to make trouble in her sweet insidious way, she realized.

Suddenly Amanda had had enough of both of them, Wynne and his chummy little friend. But she was completely gracious and really rather grand, she thought smugly, as she gave Dianne a smile and said, "Now that we are nearing port, I wonder if you would excuse me? Do talk to Wynne while I gather up some of the things I'll need for the trip ashore. He's a dear, but so distracting when I'm trying to get things done."

Not waiting for a reply, she walked away, feeling a momentary glow of satisfaction at the startled expression on Wynne's face and the petulant tightening of the girl's lips. There, Amanda told herself, chalk one up for me. She was becoming just a little weary of the sly remarks from Dianne and Wynne's irritating comments. She began to walk more briskly, realizing she shouldn't have allowed herself to be drawn into the snippy exchange of words, but unable to resist being glad that she had.

Amanda didn't go to her room, however; she simply shifted her location away from the deck where she and Wynne had been standing, and went up above on the next deck and around to the other side of the ship to watch the slow approach of Honolulu.

Hillsides latticed with the green of trees began rising like magic out of the water, and there in the distance, the contrast of skyscrapers shafting up into the air like spearheads. Amanda watched, almost breathless, her hands clenched on the railing, eyes taking in the unbelievable blue sea and the luxurious tropical growth. Suddenly the sharp memory of her mother and father blurred the achingly beautiful vision in front of her. How they had talked about coming into Hawaii by sea! She blinked away the tears, gazing now for them as well as for herself.

It was only as the ship began pushing nudgingly into the dock that Amanda could force herself to go below to get ready for the sight-seeing tour she had already planned and paid for before leaving home.

At her stateroom she knocked, the door opened at once, and Wynne stood there, a most peculiar expression on his face. She paid no attention but brushed past him, excusing herself politely, to go over and open the closet.

He shut the door. "I thought you were coming down here a long time ago."

"Oh? Well, I didn't. I wanted to see our arrival in Honolulu." She was busy sliding hangers along the rack, searching for the outfit she wanted.

"Now I suppose you want me out of the way, so I won't *distract* you?" He was ironic.

"Please." She turned her head to give him a cool polite smile. "Would you mind?"

For a moment he almost glared at her, then turned and stalked the few steps toward the door, the effectiveness hampered by the short distance. Before going out, he halted. "I'm not going on the bus tour, you know."

She nodded. "Perfectly all right. The purser doesn't expect you to accompany me everywhere, I'm sure."

He stood another moment without speaking, then deliberately closed the door firmly behind him, and his footsteps sounded down the hallway.

There was a last-minute bustle and confusion as the ship's loudspeaker began announcing the arrival of the tour buses, directions to passengers; then came the exciting scurry up the gangway and out into the fragrant humid air of Honolulu. Sidewalk merchants enticingly held out leis of ginger, frangipani, and unfamiliar blossoms in a riot of color. Amanda looked at them longingly as she was almost shoved along by the other people heading for the tour bus. For a moment she almost wished she had decided to wander about alone, but the time here was to be brief, the city so large and sprawling, she knew she had chosen wisely. All the same, she took eager looks down at the tree-lined streets and the blaze of colored blooms hanging from branches or spraying out from shrubbery.

The bus was filling and Amanda found a seat toward the rear. In a moment, a slight, elderly woman whom Amanda had glimpsed about the ship paused at her side.

"Would you mind, my dear? Unless you are expecting someone?" She nodded at the empty space next to Amanda.

"Not at all." Amanda started to rise. "Wouldn't you like this one next to the window?"

But the woman had slipped into the aisle seat quickly. "Oh, no, please stay as you are. I've made this trip many times."

She was small and frail, with skin as palely translucent as porcelain, pulled thinly over cheekbones, and with quick little blue eyes as bright as a small bird's. Wisps of white hair escaped from under a green straw hat that sat squarely on her head.

The woman touched it. "The tropical sun, you know, my dear, really quite devastating to the complexion. Not quite the latest style, but it does protect me. And we will be walking about a bit." She settled herself comfortably. "Your first trip?"

"Yes, it is." Amanda was surprised to see someone so

elderly and frail, apparently alone, traveling with such assurance.

"Your husband didn't come along today?" The green hat tilted sideways and the blue eyes gazed up at Amanda.

"Uh, no, he didn't. He was . . . busy," Amanda said uncomfortably, feeling devious and deceitful at having to lie to this pleasant elderly woman.

"Amanda . . ." the woman murmured. "How I love that name! It was my elder sister's name. One doesn't hear it much these days."

"Oh, you know my name?"

She nodded positively. "Oh, my dear, yes. Amanda Conklin. And your husband is Wynne Harrison. The passenger list, you know." She gave a quick little nod of the head, a twinkle coming into her eyes. "You must be aware that the listing does bring questions. I might say, if you don't mind, you are a topic of some interest." The woman busied herself with her purse, bringing out a small fine linen handkerchief that she used to dab at her upper lip. "Quite warm, isn't it?"

Amanda was not to be distracted. "You said, 'a topic of some interest.' May I ask why? Because of the listing?"

The woman put her handkerchief back into her purse and looked up with a smile. "Oh, my dear, it means nothing. Gossip is the handmaiden of ship's passengers. They grow bored of themselves and find interest in the most minor of things. Such as the listing of the others aboard. Why the two names, they ask? I told Mrs. Hildebrand it was the modern way, to retain one's own name. It is, isn't it, my dear?"

Amanda found herself nodding dazedly. "Yes, yes, it is."

"Of course, Mrs. Hildebrand—such a stupid old woman, you know—insists that you are not married, that you don't even wear a ring, or that, if you are married, keeping your own name is contrary to the teachings of the Bible. She quoted me some verses from the Good Book, all most irrelevant, of course." The woman smiled and said cheerfully, "I just told her that was utter nonsense. I said, 'Mrs. Hildebrand, you aren't with it!' That's correct, isn't it, doesn't one say 'with it' these days?"

Amanda felt as if she had somehow stepped through the Looking Glass and was talking to the White Queen. And she was at a complete loss for words. It didn't seem to matter; the woman was chatting comfortably on.

"Now, don't think I'm being officious, my dear ... I must call you Amanda, such a lovely name, I'm old enough to be your grandmother"—the white head nodded—"even your great-grandmother, but may I give you a little advice? Wear your ring, not for people like Mrs. Hildebrand, but for you. It's a sign of a tender bond. And someday I do hope you will take his name, or he could take yours, I'm not that old-fashioned, but someday when the little ones come along, it will be less confusing for everyone." She looked brightly at Amanda.

Amanda wondered if she had been sitting there with her mouth open; she closed her lips together, just in case. She had the feeling she was sitting in the path of a gentle, irresistible current of sound. The voice was sweet, light, and entirely friendly. One couldn't possibly take offense at the earnest sincerity, the benevolent tone.

The woman settled back in her seat comfortably, the thin pale hands, through which the bone structure showed, clasped about the large handbag, her eyes serenely watching the passing scenery.

Amanda swallowed gratefully, she needed a little respite. Her eyes were delighted by blooms of hibiscus and the bright fronds of the shower trees that the tour guide was pointing out. Ahead of them rose the craggy profile of Diamond Head.

The elderly woman leaned forward to tap Amanda on the arm. "It's not really Diamond Head. It's true name is Leahi, which means brow of the *ahi*, I suppose because it resembles the outline of the tuna, the *ahi*, as the natives call it."

Amanda pressed her face to the glass window of the bus to peer at the rugged rock. "I wonder how it ever got the name of Diamond Head, it really doesn't seem diamond-shaped."

Her companion was ready. "How clever of you to pick up that incongruous name and wonder about it; so few tourists give it a second thought. It got that name because in the nineteenth century some sailors scooped up volcanic crystals and mistook them for diamonds."

Amanda turned back to look at her companion. "You really are better than the guide. Have you ever lived in Hawaii? You know it so well, Mrs.—" She hesitated, realizing that she hadn't the faintest idea of the woman's name.

"Oh, dear! Forgive me, Amanda; how thoughtless I have been! I haven't introduced myself. I'm Sarah Jane Stewart, Mrs. My husband died in 1944, and I've been a widow all this time." The blue eyes shaded momentarily. "So I travel. Can you believe it, I made this same trip six months ago! Better than rusting away in an old folks' home back in Minneapolis." The cheerful smile was back.

The tour took them past sparkling beaches toward a palm-fringed bay that once was a crater, now opening to the sea. Amanda gazed with awe at the varied coloring of the water, emerald green over the channels, a glorious purple over the coral, and a deep endless blue beyond the reef.

"It's so beautiful," she said to Mrs. Stewart, her eyes shining.

"It is indeed," the woman said with a proud proprietary air.

It was on the tag end of the day's tour that the woman startled Amanda by saying, "You don't mind, do you, Amanda, about the stateroom you are in?"

The girl's eyes widened suddenly. She was quite uncertain how to reply. What about the room?

Mrs. Stewart noticed Amanda's surprised look, saying, "But you are in stateroom 224, aren't you?"

Amanda nodded. "Yes, but . . . I don't think I understand." What was on the woman's mind? She was speaking so oddly, so curiously.

"Oh, dear, you don't know! Maybe I shouldn't have mentioned it! I thought you knew about the two men."

"The two men?" Amanda repeated the words uncertainly.

"Oh, dear, I should never have said anything. I simply presumed you knew and didn't mind, that you weren't superstitious or anything like that." The green hat bobbed as if underlining her words.

"But . . . what about the two men? You simply can't leave the sentence like that." Amanda tried to put lightness in her voice, but underneath, she had an uneasy feeling of presentiment.

"I suppose you are right, but I really shouldn't have spoken so foolishly, without realizing you might not be aware. It really isn't anything to be afraid of. It was only"—she paused to look at Amanda apologetically—"well, on the last two trips of our ship, things happened. First trip . . . well, it was very unpleasant, very. Especially for the captain, poor man, first homicide in his career, at least it was assumed it was a homicide. A little blood was found on the floor. But they never found the man."

Amanda was staring at Mrs. Stewart, who was chatting so rapidly, bounding from word to word, leaving out details that prodded at Amanda.

"But ... what man? Why?" she asked helplessly, trying to weave together the little tag ends of the woman's disconcerting phrases.

"His name? I don't know. But one of the ship's officers told me the person was some sort of criminal type. He had quite a"—Mrs. Stewart frowned for an instant and then came up with the words triumphantly—"a 'rap-sheet' I believe, the police wanted him in the States for questioning."

"And quite frankly, Amanda"—the birdlike eyes were shrewd—"I personally think it was a 'hit man,' that's another criminal. I keep up on all these things, I do like to read detective stories, and I think that's what happened. This hit man was after him, knocked him on the head, then threw him overboard, late at night when no one was around to see. Anyhow, no one ever saw him again, the occupant from 224, he was there one day and gone the next."

Mrs. Stewart opened her purse and pulled out a little plastic box of peppermints, offering it to Amanda. "I always carry these. Most refreshing. Have one, my dear."

Thanking her, Amanda reached out, took one, popping it unconsciously into her mouth until the bite of the flavor brought her to attention. Now, why did I do that, she wondered; I hate peppermint, but this woman has me so confused.

"But you said there were two men, or two trips?" she asked the woman.

"Oh, yes. On the last trip a man in the same room, your room, was arrested. Arrested!" The colorless eyebrows raised. "Very exciting. They took him to . . . I think they call it a brig, don't they, on board ship? Yes, I should think that is the proper word," she said with maddening distraction.

"Why was he arrested? What did he do?"

"Oh, I don't know. He was taken ashore at the first port, and I never heard anything more. We were gone from the States for some time on the cruise," she explained. "If it came out in the papers, we weren't there to read it. But isn't that a strange, strange coincidence? One after another, both from the same stateroom? I was most curious to find out who would be occupying it this time. Thankfully it's a nice couple." She beamed at Amanda, then once again looked apologetic. "I do hope I haven't upset you with this silly tale."

"Oh, of course not. And I agree, it is curious," Amanda replied casually. But, inside, she didn't feel at all casual. Coincidence? Maybe, but Mrs. Stewart's breathless interest and her manner of imparting the information were enough to startle the imagination and start one suspecting something evil hung over that stateroom. Nonsense! Amanda pushed back the soft hair from her face in a nervous motion. Ridiculously, a damp cold trickle of nerves ran between her shoulders, despite the heat of the day.

She chided herself. She had been affected, she was certain, because of the candid eyes and positive little voice of her companion. Of course, it was nothing but coincidence.

The tour bus drew up at a teahouse at the top of a winding tree-lined road. The passengers filed out, Amanda giving a gentle hand to the frail woman beside her. Outside, the sun was hidden by the heavy basketwork of entwining branches and vines. Amanda wandered about in the strange and twisting tropical growth, the lush and almost overpowering moist woody scent gradually erasing the uneasiness that had temporarily bothered her.

After tea, the passengers climbed back into the bus and they began their return to the ship. Mrs. Stewart

leaned back in her seat, head against the gray upholstery, eyes beginning to droop like a sleepy infant's. Her
head tilted a bit sideways, sending the hat into a rakish
angle, and she slept, once in a while giving the gentlest
of sounds that only by imagination could be called a
snore.

Amanda felt guilty relief at the chance of a quiet time
to go back over some of the woman's strange statements.
But, no, she reminded herself, no more dwelling on macabre happenstance. So she contented herself with a languid gaze out the window as the rich tropical landscape
slipped past.

When the bus rolled up to the side of the ship, the
passengers began gathering up cameras and binoculars,
calling to one another jovially, crowding forward into
the narrow aisle. Mrs. Stewart had awakened the moment the bus stopped, and she sat upright, reaching up
her pale, veined hand to straighten the green hat.

"I must have dropped off for a moment," she said,
smiling sheepishly at Amanda. Together they made their
way out of the bus and walked slowly to the gangway,
Amanda touching her hand to the woman's elbow as
they went up the steps.

As they parted, Mrs. Stewart shook a finger at
Amanda. "Remember, my dear, an old woman's advice
. . . do consider wearing your ring. Such a lovely sentiment." A sweet smile, a coy little shake of the head, and
she went spryly off in the opposite direction.

Amanda walked slowly down the hall toward her
stateroom. She wondered where Graham had spent the
day; he had not planned on any of the tours, he told her.
He'd made them before. And her wild Irish roommate?
Had he and Dianne slipped away on some secret tryst?
Not that it mattered, she reminded herself tranquilly,
she couldn't care less what he did.

Outside her stateroom door she paused, lifting her

hand to knock, in case Wynne might be inside. Then she halted, her fist stopping in midair. From within the room came the staccato sound of drawers opening and closing rapidly, one after another, almost as if someone were searching for something. She cocked her head to one side, listening, a puzzled frown spreading across her brow. There it was again, open, shut, open, shut. And closer to the door now, almost where her drawers were located. Surely not the room steward, but if not, who was inside? Wynne? But why would he be doing this? But if not Wynne . . . ? She hesitated, uncertainly, throat gone suddenly dry.

Then, summoning up her courage, she knocked twice, lightly.

The door clicked open and Wynne stood there, a most unreadable expression on his face. She had the odd feeling she had indeed interrupted something, but he was blandly standing aside for her to enter. Her quick glance indicated everything in place. Perhaps, after all, he had been only going through his own things and her newly awakened sensitivity about the room itself supplied the rest.

"You're back earlier than I expected," he said.

Too much earlier? There, she was doing it again, she chided herself. She was simply going to have to put Mrs. Stewart's grisly tale from her mind.

He was looking at her, waiting for her to answer. "Early?" she parroted blankly. "I don't think so. It really seemed like quite a long trip. But I enjoyed it." Her eyes unconsciously began a search for signs of the possible bloodstain the woman had mentioned. Somehow, her imagination presented her with the faintest outline of an almost invisible circle.

She glanced up to find him watching her. "What's the matter, roommate? You look like you're seeing ghosts," he said.

Amanda decided she might as well out with it, for the troubling thought was apparently going to stick in her mind like a burr.

"Do you know anything, or have you heard anything, about a man, two men, really, who occupied this stateroom on former trips?"

For a moment she thought either he hadn't heard or he didn't understand what she was saying, for there was no expression on his face at all.

Then he said slowly, "Man? Men?"

"Yes, Mrs. Stewart, one of the passengers, was telling me what happened, or what she knew of what happened. Two trips ago, one man was murdered—vanished, anyway. Last trip, a man was arrested."

"For what reason, either one, I mean?"

"Well, she said she didn't know. She told me they thought the man, the first one"—she hesitated, curling a bit inside—"that he was killed here, in this very room. They found blood, but not the man. Ever."

"Which woman told you?"

"She's one of the passengers and sat next to me on the tour bus today. Quite elderly and frail. She was on the former trips, too. I have the feeling she more or less considers the ship her second home. But she was quite serious about what she was telling me."

He picked up a pen he had left lying on the dressing table and stuck it in his pocket. "Not to be rude," he said blandly, "but it's been my experience in the travel business that elderly women, often with vivid imagination and too much idle time, come up with some pretty strange tales. Not that it couldn't be true, I suppose. People have occasionally been taken into custody while abroad ship, usually for fleeing indictment. And people have been known, though rarely, to have fallen from a ship, suddenly seized with vertigo. Or once, I recall, a suicide. But two mysteries in succession—a bit much, wouldn't you think?" He was looking faintly amused now.

Amanda felt a strange reluctance to admit he could be right, somehow Mrs. Stewart had seemed so sure. "I suppose so," she said slowly. "You haven't heard any such thing?"

"No, but"—his grin suddenly flashed—"my friend Dianne hasn't been discussing such gruesome subjects with me. She leans more to the personal, if I might be so vain." He was lightly teasing, and she felt a flicker of resentment that his words momentarily bothered her. She didn't care what they talked about. The thought was firmly pushed from her mind.

At dinner that night Wynne was less talkative than usual, Amanda feeling his eyes speculatively upon her from time to time. What went on in that mind of his, she wondered? But he was pleasant enough, and Dianne and the Babcocks, the young couple who had replaced the Hildebrands, carried on a spirited conversation with Joan, the Australian girl. The conversation veered to shipboard entertainment, and Dianne turned toward Amanda, the girl's long eyelashes fluttering and revealing a challenging look the others at the table could not see.

"And you, Amanda Conklin, why is it that you never appear for the dancing each evening in the lounge? Don't you dance, or are you fearful of exposing this handsome man of yours to the wiles of all we poor spinsters?" A bold smile curved the full red lips.

Amanda felt her fingers curl tightly in her lap. Again she thought of how the red-haired girl's impudence would hurt were she really married to Wynne. For there was a streak of brashness and sly taunting in the girl's seemingly innocent remarks.

"Dance?" Amanda said smoothly. "I do, indeed. It's only that there has been so much else to do, we haven't yet managed the evening dances. Isn't that right, Wynne?" She turned innocent eyes toward him. This was his girlfriend, let him handle it.

She saw his mouth twitch, but he said placidly, "Quite right. I'm sure we'll make it sooner or later."

After dinner, Wynne excused himself and said he'd see her later, he wanted to run into downtown Honolulu. He grinned at her, said, "Don't bother to wait up," and was gone before she could make any reply.

Amanda strolled about on deck for a while, watching the sparkle of nighttime Honolulu, the reflection of the ship's lights on the water, and above, a moon so large and golden it looked artificial. But eventually she tired of walking and, feeling restless, went down to the movie in the ship's theater.

The film had been going but a few moments when Graham slipped into the seat beside her.

"Hello, beautiful, I've missed you all day. Damn, I should have taken the tour," he whispered.

There was a stern shushing from in back of them, and Graham settled back in his seat, reaching over quietly to take her hand in his.

Amanda felt terribly self-conscious all at once. It was a harmless affectionate gesture on his part, but her hand felt stiff and awkward. To draw it away would be even more awkward, so she sat watching the film, uncomfortably aware that she did not want him holding her hand. Why, she had no idea. She liked him, he was charming, pleasant, certainly attractive. Then why . . . ?

Suddenly chagrin flowed over her, and she felt a hot flush rushing to her face there in the dark. How stupid! How absolutely ridiculous! She couldn't bear to admit to herself that the secret reason was that it made her feel oddly guilty of infidelity. She bit down on her lower lip angrily until the sudden hurt made her release it. Dummy! she thought violently, she was a mindless simpleton. Very well, let Graham hold her hand if he wanted to. Fine! She sat there rigidly, her hand reaching out, as cold and unfeeling as a china doll's.

After the movie they strolled about the deck, gazing at the city sparkling in the dark.

"We should have gone into town," he said regretfully. "In a place that size we certainly wouldn't be observed by the ship's passengers, if that's important to you. We could have had dinner and a whole evening together instead of an innocuous stroll about the deck."

She paused by the railing to lean upon it, watching the pattern of reflections on the satiny water. "I suppose we could have, but maybe it's just as well."

"Frankly, Amanda"—he leaned close to her—"I think this whole thing is ridiculous. No one has a right to toss you off the ship just because you aren't married. You have a right to that room, and if I were you, I'd push the case. It isn't too late, you know. You were in it first and you can make a stand now. We'll be in port until late tomorrow afternoon, why not try to do something about it? The present situation puts a cloud over your whole trip, it hampers you"—his voice grew intimate—"hampers me, I should say."

Suddenly his arms were around her and he pulled her to him gently. Before she could protest, he had lifted her chin with a finger and tilted her head up, coming down on her lips with a quick ardent kiss.

She drew back, startled, but not before she heard footsteps retreating rapidly in back of them.

"I—you shouldn't," she said falteringly. "I—we—" The words trailed away, her mind confused.

"Never mind, Amanda, darling," he said softly. "We're in the shadows here. No one could see us, if that worries you. This is just what I mean. Break off the crazy arrangement."

"I heard someone. They—" she began tensely, her lips

still conscious of the sudden pressure of his, and not at all certain it was pleasing. She couldn't sort out her emotions.

"Ship's crew," he cut in smoothly. "No doubt a deckhand. Doesn't know us, used to seeing romantic couples." Abruptly he chuckled, locking his arm in hers and tightening his hold. "This is the damnedest way to romance a girl I ever heard of. All the inherent dangers of cuckoldry and"—he paused significantly—"and none of the pleasures, if I might venture to say so."

With that, she pulled away, but he was quick to grasp her arm again. "I'm sorry, Amanda, that slipped out. I apologize."

He sounded so repentant that she felt silly in making any further issue of it, but settled the matter by saying she really ought to be going below to go to bed, it had been a long day and the unacustomed humidity tired her. If it was all a bit evasive, it was the only thing she could think of. And she did feel suddenly weary and low-spirited.

"Where's Harrison tonight?" he asked curiously as they walked along the deck toward the door.

"In town. He'll be back later," she said slowly, her mind nudging her with the thought that no doubt he hadn't gone alone.

At the door of the lounge they parted, at Amanda's suggestion. He gave a final squeeze to her hand as she said, "Good night," and left, going down the steps, then the long hall to her stateroom.

It was empty. Wynne had not returned, not yet. Slowly she prepared for bed behind the closed door of the bathroom, routinely rubbing cream into her face, her eyes focused unseeingly on the mirror. Graham was not to be tossed aside idly, she realized. A week ago she would have been delighted to have the attention of so attractive a man. She should be now. Somehow, she was not.

Amanda had no more than slipped into bed when there was the faint knock, then the key, and the door opened and Wynne came in. She had not yet had time to extinguish her light and he turned to look at her curiously. "I didn't expect to find you in so soon," he said coolly.

"I didn't go anywhere . . . except to the movie," she replied, surprised to find her voice tart.

"Not that I care, Amanda, nor is it any of my business"—he gave her an oblique look—"but don't you think the open deck is a rather public place to carry on your little embraces?"

So he had been the one who had walked away! "You are quite right; it is not your business!" she retorted hotly, sinking back hard into her pillow, covers pulled up to her chin, glaring at him.

"That's what I said. But as your ersatz husband, I thought it appropriate to register some sort of protest," he said cheerfully. With that, he began stripping off his jacket, hanging it in the closet. She watched as he calmly sauntered into the bathroom, locking the door in that loud pointed way.

Reaching up, she flicked off her light and lay back on the pillow once more, lips compressed. Why should she care what he said, what he had seen? She clenched her fingers around the top of the sheet she still had pulled up to her chin. Shutting her eyes tightly, she willed herself to sleep. When the click of the lock came moments later, they flew open again involuntarily. She had a glimpse of his tall, pajama-clad figure outlined against the light of the bathroom before she closed her eyes again, her heart pounding giddily.

Propinquity, that's what he had warned her about, she reminded herself distractedly, this being together in such an intimate situation. No wonder she was reacting with unsteady breath and ridiculously racing pulse.

The light clicked in the bathroom, then came the creak of the ladder as he climbed to the top bunk and settled down, pounding his pillow noisily, yawning. Then he flipped off the light, sending the small room into darkness.

Suddenly he spoke. "Good night, Amanda. Don't let thoughts about the ghosts of past occupants disturb your dreams."

"Thanks . . . thanks a lot," she said bitterly. "That's all it will take to set me thinking of them again."

"I'm sorry." He actually sounded contrite. "That was meant as a joke. Forget about all that bunk you heard, for that's all it is—bunk. Ship's gossip can bend things all out of shape."

Strange how intimate an ordinary conversation became in the dark, Amanda reflected. For a long time she lay there, silent, listening to the slow steady breathing of the man sleeping a foot or two away. What an uncanny feeling!

She really hadn't needed the mention of the two men who had once occupied this room to keep her awake. They had been lurking in the back of her thoughts for some time now. She stared into the dark, trying to brush them from her mind, seeking for drowsiness that kept eluding her.

Finally she did sleep, an unhappy, troubled dream pursuing her through the next hours. It was like looking down into a deep shadowed pit, seeing faces moving, fading, appearing again. Harry Shields' small eyes haunted her as she tossed, restless and nightmarish.

Morning found her still weary. She struggled up on one elbow to gaze speculatively again at that faint suspicious spot on the carpet. Then her eyes lifted, the bathroom door was open. Had he shaved and gone already? She felt on the floor with her foot, seeking her slippers, then slid her feet into them. Grasping her robe, she knotted the belt about her.

She had almost reached the bathroom door, today's clothes clutched in her hand, when Wynne's voice intercepted her.

"Good lord! I overslept, meant to be up early. Going back into town until we sail."

Amanda turned. He was sitting up in his bunk, rubbing his head vigorously with a knotted fist.

"Say, Amanda, you know, you don't look like an ice maiden now, with your face all rosy from sleep and your hair every which way." He was grinning broadly. "Really quite an improvement, if you ask me."

She didn't reply; she marched into the bathroom, followed by the sound of his chuckle. "Damn the man!" she muttered into her toothbrush. Why did she let him irritate her so easily? She was simply overreacting to everything. Suddenly she met her eyes in the mirror and stared unbelievingly. No! Not that! It couldn't possibly be! Why—why—she didn't like him very much at all, did she?

Amanda turned her head toward the closed door of the bathroom. He had made it clear, right from the very beginning. No time for romance, he had warned her ... beware of propinquity. Except, she reflected miserably, except with that red-haired menace.

This was sheer nonsense. She glowered at herself in the mirror. She hadn't fallen in love with that . . . that man out there in the other room! No, it was only the forced intimacy of housing, the constant emphasis of their odd situation. Amanda lowered her toothbrush, firming her jaw stubbornly. Whatever she might feel about him, she was not going to allow him to suspect that she wasn't simply putting up with an unexpected cir-

cumstance. He could just think that she was interested
in Graham.

She hesitated at that thought. She mustn't encourage
Graham; it wouldn't be fair, and she had the uneasy
feeling that Graham might misunderstand any encouragement. The situation between them was already
showing signs of being a bit of a problem.

She dressed quickly, brushing her hair smoothly into
place, then went out into the room. As she entered, he
was propped up in his bed, reading. He lifted his eyes.

"There, back to the ice maiden, more like the roommate I have grown to know and fear. And respect, yes,
indeed." He gave her a brisk salute. "Yes, ma'am! By the
way, I won't be having breakfast with you. I'm going on
into town right away. But," he said, with a half-grin, "I'll
be back in time to sail with the ship, just in case you
were getting your hopes up that I'd miss it."

"I was. Perhaps there will be a cancellation and one of
us can move into it," she replied calmly, picking up her
purse to stick a small bottle of suntan lotion inside.

"Sure, we could approach the purser again and say
that we had another fight . . . or that you were going to
divorce me and didn't want to spend any more time in
my presence. Better have the story ready, just in case
the opportunity to move arises."

Was he serious? She couldn't tell. She simply told him
she was going to the dining room now and would see
him, she supposed, later. They could settle the room
question then, if there should be an opening.

Going down the hall, she wondered how she honestly
felt about the situation, the possibility of either one of
them moving into another stateroom. She'd prefer it. Of
course she would! She was beginning to have doubts
about what might occur to her emotions should the
present situation continue. It wasn't that she might fall

in love with him, not that at all, she reassured herself firmly. But, she might *think* she was.

After breakfast she caught a glimpse of Graham strolling around on the deck below. She didn't want to see him, not right now, she decided suddenly, not after last night. Eventually, of course, she would, but at this moment she was muddled enough inside.

Hurrying back to the stateroom, empty now, she touched her lips with color, took a small amount of money from a safe hiding place in her dresser drawer, where she had tucked it in a stocking case, and left, heading for the gangway.

Out in the bright sunlight on the dock, she found a set of stone stairs leading down in a green tropical park. She felt the moist warmth of the air about her as she followed the walk through the park and out into the busy city.

It was nearly sailing time when she came hurrying back up the stairs and heading toward the ship. She had been entranced with window-shopping, spending nothing at all except for a glass of fruit juice. Wandering in and out of the stores, strolling through the streets, she was fascinated by the interesting mélange of races that made up the city, dazzled by glimpses of blazing tropical flowers.

A number of passengers had already started gathering at the ship's rail, waiting for the casting off and sailing. Amanda joined them, leaning over to watch the latecomers, who, fearful of being left behind, were glancing nervously up at the ship, scurrying up the gangway, clutching their purchases.

There was no sign of Wynne, and for a moment she wondered if he really had missed the ship. As the whistle blew, an orchestra onshore began playing "Aloha," serpentine uncoiled, and they began their slow ponderous move toward the open sea once more.

Amanda turned away to search out a deck chair where she could sit and watch the slow disappearance of Honolulu from the horizon, and she found herself fatigued from her long walk in town. But she could not bear to go below until every speck of land vanished.

She had been sitting for some time when she became aware of someone standing beside her. Wearing the familiar pink, flowered blouse that strained over the pendulous bosom was Mrs. Hildebrand, hostile eyes fixed on Amanda.

"I guess you know why Claude and I moved from your table." Without waiting for a reply, the woman said accusingly, "It's just that I can't stand seeing sin thrown in my face like that." Her face grew pinker and seemed to swell. "You don't wear a ring, seems to me you would if you had one. And if you are married, then parading around without a ring, acting like you aren't joined through eternity to someone, that's almost the same."

"Mrs. Hildebrand," Amanda began, struggled out of her chair, deciding she need not take any more of this type of attack, "I do think . . ."

But she had no time to finish. The woman had gripped her wrist, not hard, but firmly, "I always say, hate the sin but love the sinner. I don't mind telling you that sometimes it's pretty hard." She let the wrist go. "It's not too late to change your ways, Amanda *Conklin,* you can become a decent woman, not a strumpet." With that she walked off, leaving a shaken Amanda in her wake.

Amanda flung around and hurried down the deck to the far end of the ship, breathing hard, knees trembling. That dreadful, dreadful woman! Those nasty insinuations! They cut at her as she stood, hands gripping the rail, tears stinging her eyelids. And it wasn't made easier by the realization that the woman was right about one thing: she wasn't married. And she was making the trip in the same stateroom with a man who wasn't married, either.

The wind was whipping up slightly now, the humid air of the island slowly being absorbed by the motion of the ship through the cool spray of the sea. Amanda took several deep, steadying breaths, trying to calm herself. She looked down at her left hand. The last thing in the world she would have wanted was to admit she could picture a plain golden band there. She shook herself; she was allowing herself to be dragged into a wicked deceptive trap. Mrs. Hildebrand's biting comments had only stirred up her feeling of disquiet that had seized her this morning.

Joan, the girl from Australia, came around the corner and walked up to Amanda. Her plain strong face was serious.

"I saw Mrs. Hildebrand talking to you down at the other end of the ship and I could tell she was upsetting you, Amanda. Don't pay any attention to her; she's a real tartar, and we're all glad she and that poor husband of hers have moved to another table. I suppose she was on to you about your own name or not wearing a ring. The old trout!" Joan scowled. "She runs around quoting the Bible to everyone, and the old stove hasn't an iota of real Christian spirit in that overfed body of hers."

Abraded as her inner feelings were, Amanda found a smile curving her lips at Joan's fierce expression and explosive words. "She was finding me on the sinner's list, no matter what category of marriage, or no marriage, I was claiming," she said ruefully.

Joan cast a scathing look in the general direction of the ship's area where the confrontation between Mrs. Hildebrand and Amanda had taken place. "Amanda, it's no one's business how you conduct your own life. If it

does no one any harm, then why give a thought to the
Mrs. Hildebrands of this world?"

Amanda looked warmly at Joan. The girl had said the
one thing that could make her feel better. "If it does no
one any harm." After all, who was hurt by this silly pre-
tense? No one. How carefully she skirted the possibility
that there might eventually be *one* . . . her own self. She
must not let herself be tricked by her emotions into even
thinking she cared for that unconcerned, nonchalant
man who shared her room.

The two girls walked along the deck, talking idly now,
until someone called down to Joan from the upper deck,
reminding her of a quick game of shuffleboard before
dinner. Joan turned to Amanda. "Remember now, don't
fret about Mrs. Hildebrand and her nasty old mind and
tongue."

"I won't . . . from now on. At least I'll try not to,"
Amanda said wistfully. "And . . . thanks, Joan."

The other girl lifted a hand in farewell as she started
for the stairs. "Cheerio, Amanda; see you at dinner."

Amanda walked thoughtfully back to her stateroom,
looking up to speak to other passengers who greeted her
as they passed by in the long hall. Letting herself into
her room, she pulled off her neck scarf and tugged open
her dresser drawer to put it away, then shut the drawer
with the tiny slam she found was necessary on shipboard. She halted, the sound tugging at her mind. That
was what she had heard yesterday when she had come
to the door and Wynne was inside. She pulled out the
drawer and shut it once again, rapidly, then the next
drawer. Yes, that was exactly it, drawer after drawer.

She frowned, pursing her lips. And hadn't she thought
that some of the slams had come pretty close to the door
side—in other words, from her side? But her uncertain
feeling at the time had been diverted by the ensuing

conversation about the two men who had once inhabited this room.

Had Wynne been looking for something? Not just among his possessions, but also among hers? Slowly she pulled out the drawer again, running her hand experimentally over the clothes on top, under the clothes, along the bottom. Nothing, nothing at all, but she hadn't really expected there would be. If, indeed, he had been searching for an object, it would have to be small; otherwise she would have seen it anytime she opened the drawer.

She stood there, feeling a little overdramatic, a bit silly about the whole thing, yet not quite able to shrug it from her thoughts. Almost reluctantly she reached out again, pulling out another drawer, staring down at it. Abruptly her eyes widened; she stiffened.

There, its pink satin cover showing from under a neatly arranged pile of blouses, was her stocking case. She had so cautiously placed it at the very bottom, between two slips, when she had left to go into Honolulu earlier. Now it was out of place. Her money! Her precious small horde of spending money for the entire trip. So little, but so needed. Her mouth went dry as she picked up the hosiery folder with a trembling hand, opened it, and was immediately swept with a cold wave of perspiration—but one of relief. Her money was all there, her fingers quickly ran through it. Every single dollar bill!

She clutched the folder in nerveless fingers. Someone had been in that drawer since she had left. Someone who had carefully left everything undisturbed, yet inadvertently made a mistake in misplacing this small satin case. She lifted her eyes to stare in the mirror, not even seeing her reflection. *Who?* Who else could it be but Wynne? Only yesterday she had heard— Her lips tightened and a rush of anger flooded over her. How dared he go through her things?

At that moment there was a knock at the door, and she turned abruptly to jerk it open, eyes blazing.

Wynne grinned cheerfully at her as he sidled past. "Have a good time today?"

"Have a good search of my things today?" she snapped.

He actually seemed surprised, or he was a very good actor, she thought uncertainly. But who else . . . ?

For a moment he seemed to hesitate, then said slowly, "I? I searched your things? Nothing of the sort. What's missing?"

"What did you find?" her voice crackled. It had to be Wynne, for only yesterday . . .

"Find? How could I find anything? I didn't touch your things." The blue eyes darkened until they were almost black, a tinge of red creeping up his neck and into his face. "Now, just a damned minute, Miss Priss, why would I want anything of yours?"

"Don't try to evade the question." Her fingers curled tightly at her side. "You see, I heard you yesterday. You were opening drawers, one after another. Including mine, I think. What are you looking for? I'd hate to think you were a common thief." She looked at him steadily. "But if you aren't, then something very queer is going on. I want to know what."

The look of irritation slowly drained from his face; he looked at her speculatively, rubbing at the edge of his jaw with his hand for a long moment before he spoke, this time in a completely different tone. "Amanda, are you certain someone has been into your things today? I don't mean *think*, are you absolutely sure?"

She nodded, now a bit disconcerted at the intensity of his question. "Yes. No doubt of it. I heard you yesterday so that's why I knew . . ." She hesitated, then rephrased the sentence. "I thought it was you again."

He stepped over to sink down on the sofa, hands clasped behind his head, eyes thoughtful, legs stretched out in front of him. He didn't speak.

"Well," she said, "was it you?" She still wasn't certain.

"I'm not to blame. I've been ashore all day." He seemed remote, his thoughts clearly on another path even as he spoke absently.

"But you were going through the drawers, all of them, even mine, yesterday?" she persisted stubbornly.

He was suddenly still, then lifted his eyes, looking at her with an odd myopic stare. Abruptly he seemed to bring his thoughts back with a jerk. "All right, I was looking for something. Nothing of yours. Something that was lost." There was the beginning of irritation and impatience creeping into his voice now. "Let's just say it was— Well, I'm not to blame for today."

Now his eyes narrowed and he sat as if his thoughts were involved in a world she was not to enter.

Impulsively she spoke. "Wynne, what's going on? Something is. Don't you think I have a right to ask? This is my room, too, you know." Suddenly she felt a feather-light finger of fear. "There's too much that's unnerving about the whole thing. All the mystery about the two men in this room on the two previous trips. Now you—and if you are telling the truth, someone else—going through drawers, trying to find something. What, Wynne, why?" Her voice had steadied now and was demanding.

He gave an impatient sigh. "Oh, hell, I should have expected something like this to happen. I can see trouble ahead. That is, if you are going to bumble around asking questions you shouldn't be asking. If things had gone right, I'd have had this room alone and no questions, no problems."

He looked completely exasperated, but finally nodded in a reluctant manner. "Oh, okay, I suppose you are right. Maybe I ought to explain . . . a little anyhow. You really shouldn't know, of course. Sit down and I'll tell you what I can. Confess." He gave her a bitter smile.

She sat down beside him, but far enough away so that she wouldn't be physically aware of his nearness. "Very well, Wynne, what is it?"

He started to speak, appeared to reconsider, then shrugged. "It's a long story. I'm looking for something. And, if you are right about your things having been searched, it hasn't been found. Not yet."

"It?"

"A key. A small ordinary key. Or a note, or some indication of where what we're looking for may be. It's . . ." He looked disgruntled but continued grudgingly, "Remember the Carleton and Sims robbery a year ago? The unbelievable haul in diamonds the thieves got away with?"

"The New York jewelry store? I read about it. But they caught the robber, didn't they?"

"There were four. One, yes, they caught one." He paused as if uncertain whether or not to go ahead, then added slowly, "But only one. On board this ship."

"In this room." Amanda didn't even bother to put it in the form of a question.

"In this room.

"One," he went on after a pause, "one died."

She looked at him, her heart giving an uncontrollable twisting jump. Then her eyes turned toward the place on the rug, or what she thought was once a stain. Then she raised her head.

He shrugged and nodded.

There was an abrupt rap at the door, sending Amanda's nerves into knots. She jerked, stretching out her hand to tighten suddenly on Wynne's arm. She swallowed once, hard. "It's—it's—" Her voice dwindled to a stop.

He looked down at her hand, gently removed it from his arm, stood up, and opened the door. A steward held out a radiogram. "For you, Mr. Harrison."

Wynne shut the door and sat down. "Do you mind?" He held up the wire.

"No, go ahead." How foolish she felt, panicking like that at a simple knock on the door.

He glanced at the message, replaced it in the envelope, and tucked in an inner pocket of his jacket.

"Wynne, you've told me only enough to make it even more puzzling. And disturbing. There's more."

"There's more," he said resignedly. "And no matter what I decide to do, it'll be the wrong thing, count on that. I can see that. Very well, I work for an insurance firm, do investigations. The jewels were never recovered. We got a roundabout tip that they were stashed away somewhere by one of the men, to be picked up and shared later when the heat was off. Only, it seems like the guy decided to run out on the other three, disappear, maybe figuring to come back later on the quiet, pick up the loot, and keep it for himself. Bought a one-way ticket to Australia, then boarded this ship."

Amanda watched Wynne as he spoke. "And someone found out and caught up with him, here on board?" she asked tensely.

He nodded. "But he must have had something with him, some sort of lead to what he had hidden. I guess they didn't find it and so on the very next trip, one of the others got the same stateroom, no doubt intent on locating what was not discovered after the murder. But the cops caught up with him first. That leaves two to go. It also"—he glanced around the room—"leaves this stateroom. Everything points to the fact that whatever it is, is still here."

Her eyes followed his around the room. "But you looked?"

He nodded, then the twisted grin came again. "As you caught me doing by listening outside the door yesterday."

A troubling thought began to creep up on her, lifting the hairs coldly along her arm. "But if you didn't"—she motioned vaguely with her hand at the drawer—"then who did today?"

He gave her a level look. "There are still two of them."

"You don't know who they are, what they look like, their names?"

He shook his head. "Farnum won't talk; he's the one picked up on the ship here. He's in prison. As for the one who went overboard, it was a little late for him to tell anyone, even if he had any last-minute inclinations. The name on the passport was Corcoran. Not his right name, of course. It was Desmond, been in jail a dozen times, a long and varied record. We have no knowledge of who the other two are. But we figured one of them would somehow manage to be on the very next sailing, this one."

Leaning back, Wynne eyed her frankly. "I must say, Amanda, I realized there was another occupant slated for this two-passenger unit. But you were a shock. I couldn't believe my luck to have gotten number 224. Until I walked out of that bathroom the first day and almost bumped into you. That stunned me."

"But couldn't you have told them you *had* to have the room to yourself? I mean, not after I had it, too, but before? They might have assigned me to another stateroom."

"Look, to all purposes, I'm an ordinary tourist. This is a two-man room, or so I thought. Two-person room, if you will. But I didn't want to make a request to have it alone, to insist, for there might be questions. And problems. There could be criminal collusion with someone connected with the ship, for all I know. Unfortunately for both of us, they must have thought I was another female, because of the name, I guess. So here we are. And I draw an inquisitive roommate."

Chapter 5

A small dark suspicion started to mushroom in her mind. "Wynne, there's a man, maybe you've seen him, he's in with Graham, across the hall." She remembered the feeling of unease the man had aroused in her. "He looks like a sort of gangster type. Could he be the one?"

Wynne lifted his shoulders in a philosophical shrug. "Who knows? I've had a look at the guy you mean. Could be. But I never guess on things like this. Appearances can be deceiving. And look, Amanda, remember I'm working on guesses. This could be all feathers in a whirlwind. Maybe one of the crooks isn't on board at all. And your drawer being searched just the work, the pilfering act of someone going through some of the cabins. He didn't find anything, so he moved on."

"Which you don't believe," she said positively.

"Which I won't completely rule out," he countered.

She had to be content with that. But she gave a swift searching look at his bland expression. Clearly nothing else was to be pried from him at the moment.

He got up, giving a restless glance around the room. "As long as you know, I might as well stop curtailing my search to periods when you are out of the room. Mind if I give another"—he sighed almost inaudibly—"look around? I feel I've covered every possibility, but I can't get over the absolute conviction that whatever it is that someone is looking for, is—or was—here."

"Was?"

"He might have found it today. Though hanged if I think I could have missed it."

"And you don't know what you're looking for?" she persisted. It seemed ridiculous. What if he came across something and didn't recognize it for what it was?

"Not precisely."

"And you aren't even positive it's here, whatever it is?" she asked curiously. "Maybe you're wasting your time."

"Maybe," he said laconically. "But our tip says it's here. My boss"—he patted the pocket containing the cable—"is even more certain."

He stood, hands on hips, scrutinizing the ceiling. Amanda looked up, too, but all she saw was plain, cream-colored surface. Wynne shook his head and sighed. "Weirdest assignment I've ever had. I should have been suspicious when my boss, who isn't given to gracious gestures, suggested I take my vacation at this time. Then he dangled the offer of this cruise in front of my eyes. The hook was to find and bring back what the robber hid. 'I don't care if it takes the whole trip, find it!' he says. 'Then, when you get it, bring it back on the double.'" Wynne gave her a wry smile. "Now the tune changes and he's beginning to put on the heat. I've looked, my God, how I've looked." His eyes began traveling about the room, the walls, the carpeting, again.

She watched him for a moment, then she stirred restlessly. "I'll leave you the place to yourself and go up on deck until time to dress for dinner. See you later."

"Sure," he murmured absently, his gaze still circling the stateroom, as if he could somehow stare out the answer.

The briskness of the sea air out on deck somewhat eased, but did not entirely sweep away the knot of tensions that lay deep inside her. A group of passengers were huddled at the rail, talking excitedly and pointing.

Amanda quickly joined them to lean over and gaze curiously at the expanse of blue water.

One of the ship's officers, a pleasant-faced, middle-aged man, was by her side. "We are seeing a school of flying fish," he explained. "There, look quick!"

Her eyes caught the sudden flutter and rise of small white objects, up from a curling swell of water; they soared for a short distance, then vanished into the sea once again.

"But they look like birds, little white birds, and they fly in a group, a formation, don't they?" She watched them wonderingly, straining her eyes to catch another glimpse. For several moments the water flowed by endlessly; then abruptly there they were again, like silver leaves caught in the sunlight, lifting their small shapes through the air.

Amanda laughed delightedly. "They are absolutely beautiful. My parents used to tell me about them when they talked of the trip they made years ago."

Again dozens of eyes searched the surface of the sea, then a chorus of "Ahs!" rose once again at the flight of the flying fish.

The officer smiled at Amanda's enthusiasm. "You know, you say they look like birds. Maybe we should say a *covey* instead of a *school* of fish."

A woman called to him; he excused himself to Amanda and went over to help the passenger adjust her camera.

"I've been looking for you." Graham was suddenly at her elbow, his eyes warm as she turned her head toward him.

"I don't think we should be seeing too much of each other, Graham," she said slowly. "After all, people do talk, and I hear that on board ship gossip passes around quickly."

"Amanda," he said quietly, "I know you aren't married, you know you aren't, and certainly your roommate knows you aren't. The devil with anyone else. And, believe me, no one is going to run to the purser. Even if they do, he's in the clear where his conscience is concerned on policy. He's not going to raise a fuss."

She slid her eyes away from his intent gaze.

"Amanda," he insisted, "why are you condemning yourself to seclusion? You are by far the most attractive girl on board ship. The trip isn't going to last forever, and I want to know you better. A lot better. Ah—ah—I know"—he fended off her attempt to speak—"I know about the stories of shipboard romances and how they fade away when the gangway goes down for the last time and the trip ends. That, my dear Amanda, isn't necessarily true."

She couldn't help feeling flattered by his attention, what girl wouldn't be, she reflected. All the same, right from the first he had been inclined to move along a little faster than she could feel comfortable about. After all, she had known him only a few days. There was a strong streak of seriousness that she was unready for yet. If ever she would be, she thought uncertainly.

His hand slipped over hers unobtrusively as it lay on the rail. Again, as in the movie, she wanted to draw it away, but waited a full moment before she gave him a smile that asked for understanding, then moved her hand, letting it fall to her side.

"Okay, little one," he said almost philosophically, "but just remember, I'm not giving up."

She glanced down at her watch. "Oh, it's later than I thought," she said hurriedly. "We're on the first sitting, you know, so it's time to start getting ready. Perhaps I'll see you later."

She started to turn from the rail when she was met by his amused eyes. "Scaredy-cat! I'll let you go this time.

Count on it, you will see me later, somewhere, and no perhaps about it. I'm not that easy to discourage."

When she reached her room, Wynne was not there, only the faint scent of shaving lotion remained as a reminder. Opening the closet, she reached for a sleeveless shift of pale pink and stepped into the bathroom to slip into the dress that she self-consciously realized was one of the most becoming that she owned. Just who was she dressing for? And why was the face reflecting back from the bathroom mirror so bright of eye and pink of cheek? The latter probably sunburn, she told herself firmly, peering sternly into the mirror, touching the faint glow with tentative fingers to see if her skin felt warm from the sun. It was not. So . . . ? Not Wynne. Certainly not Wynne. How could she even allow herself such a traitorous thought? Hadn't she, some time ago, decided to stop this type of imagining? Look at it this way, she lectured herself, what kind of man is Wynne Harrison? He's stubborn, flippant, and certainly not at all what he had at first professed to be. She picked up her hairbrush, then halted with it lifted halfway to her blond hair. He had first said he was a travel writer. Now he was some kind of investigator. So he said.

Pursing her lips thoughtfully, she turned that phrase over and over in her mind. *So he said.* Was he? Or was it something he had produced to quickly fend off her suspicion about who had been searching the dresser drawers?

Absently she began brushing her hair, a vein in her temple pulsing. She should have considered this sooner, even as he was talking to her. Why hadn't she? Was it because she'd subconsciously blocked the suspicion, not allowing it to grow?

Slowly she walked out into the other room to put her brush in the drawer. There was only one possible thing she could do now. Wait and see. Keep a sharp eye and a clear mind where Wynne Harrison was concerned.

At dinner he was as cheerful as if nothing at all had occurred in their stateroom. He joked teasingly at Dianne, sending the redhead into a flirtatious mood—if she needed the encouragement, Amanda thought coolly. The Babcocks were quick to pick up the banter, and as Joan Blakey joined the group she said, "My word, this is a jolly table."

Amanda found herself caught up in the laughter and fun, the doubts and unpleasant suspicions not entirely disappearing, but retreating quietly into the back of her mind, waiting.

"Why don't you and Wynne join us at the dance later on this evening?" Tina Babcock urged Amanda. Then her eyes moved with amusement around the table. "And we can be generous and include our two unclaimed blessings, Dianne and Joan."

Amanda wasn't certain she'd enjoy an evening of dancing with Dianne seated at the table with them. There was something about the red-haired girl that irritated her. Perhaps it was the challenge she could read from time to time in the girl's eyes. But Wynne was saying, "Sounds good to me, how about you, Amanda, dear?" That last word was delivered with the shadow of a mocking wink.

"Love it!" Amanda replied promptly. He was not going to put her in the position of being a wet blanket by refusing.

"Sure"—Wynne was leaning back in his chair—"I think it's time for us to go a little more social. How's the music?"

Lee Babcock smiled. "Not sensational, but certainly not bad. We've been up in the lounge every night, hopping around." He pushed back his chair. "See you all up there in about an hour?"

It was agreed, and gradually they all left the table. Wynne walked out of the dining room with Amanda, then out on deck with her.

"Think maybe I ought to show a little more husbandly attention," he said casually. "Our little friend Dianne is beginning to show signs of suspicion. Makes pointed little comments about seeing that guy, Graham, hanging around you. And noticing that we two aren't together often. Or ever. Except at meals. Don't want her to get any ideas. She has enough as it is, say I, modestly."

She slanted a quick glance at him. There was no discernible expression evident on his face; he simply looked relaxed and immensely unconcerned about anything.

Well, *she* was! And, in spite of herself, she said, "Wynne, first you said you were a writer, a writer of travel books, now you say you are an investigator."

"I am." Still that casual air.

"Are you a detective? A policeman?"

"A little bit of the first, none of the second. I do some detecting, if that's what you mean. My firm stands to lose one hell of a lot of money if we don't find those diamonds. They have to be somewhere. Maybe"—he lifted a quizzical eyebrow—"maybe the store staged the whole thing, claimed the loss, planned to later recut the jewels or fence them. Maybe. That's not unheard of, you know. Hired a bunch of thugs, who maybe ran out on them. Frankly, I don't know. Nobody is certain of anything except that the robbery took place, and everything leads to this ship. Why?"

The question was put sharply. "Don't you believe me yet? Still think I'm the bad guy? Could be your pal, Graham, you know. Or Babcock, or even Moore's roommate."

She felt a guilty flush warming her face. "It's just that I don't know what to think anymore. Back home in Arizona, I lead a very different kind of life. Now, here I am on a cruise, and in a few short days I find myself with a strange man as a roommate—"

"You didn't say an attractive man; I'm mortally wounded," he broke in, grinning at her.

She had the feeling he was purposely trying to distract her from the subject of the diamond theft, but she plowed stubbornly on as if he hadn't spoken. "I not only find myself considered a gossip target on my marriage status, but also discover there's a whole lot going on in which I'm involved, whether you think so or not, simply because we are occupying the same stateroom. So I want to know *truthfully* what's going on."

"Look, Amanda, I've told you the truth, whether you believe it or not. So far, there's nothing more to tell. If there is, I'll keep you posted. Sure, I know as well as you do that you've been pulled into it innocently; I'll level with you in the future." The banter was all gone from his voice.

Suddenly she felt better. And she believed him. *Now* she did. Maybe she was foolish and easily deceived, but there was a certain tone when he spoke that sounded right. The concern about the room still lingered, the nervous alarm about the intruder who had rifled through the drawer, but it was almost as if a burden had been lifted from her mind. Be honest, she told herself silently, you didn't want to disbelieve him.

For a little while they strolled silently, except to exchange good evenings with other strollers, some of whom bent benign smiles upon them.

Not everyone thinks I'm beyond all salvation, Amanda reflected. Not everyone feels like Mrs. Hildebrand.

The moon was coming up and a wide silver path spread across the dark satin of the water. Suddenly Wynne said, "You know, Amanda, you spoke a moment ago of Arizona. I know you come from there by your passport, but I don't know much more about you. We've been on such formal terms, there's been so much frostiness in the air, I didn't feel free to ask. What prompts this cruise on your part? All you would say before was to grit your teeth stubbornly and snap that you had to make the trip. This trip. Now."

She hesitated, then said slowly, "It was my parents' dream." Quietly, she told him.

"Every New Year's Eve, until they died, we would stand around the table to give a toast, they in champagne, I in ginger ale, lifting up our champagne glasses, saying, 'To our South Pacific trip.'" She looked wistfully out at the dark moving water.

For a few moments, silence fell between them; then he said, "This boss of yours sounds like Ebenezer Scrooge before the reformation. He should have given you the six weeks *with* salary, instead of sticking you with the other girl's pay for two weeks. Why didn't you tell him to keep his miserly old job? Get something else when you go back?"

"They're not that easy to find in my hometown. And I need one."

"Why isn't—if you'll forgive me," he said with a lopsided smile, "why isn't a pretty young girl like you married? Your passport says you are twenty-one— Oh, yes, I looked it over thoroughly when I turned it into the purser's office. After all, for all I knew, you could have been one of the jewel thieves, or a gangster's moll."

Amanda laughed. "Now you sound like Mrs. Stewart, the elderly lady who went on the bus tour with me. She uses criminal and police terms all the time. As for why I'm not married, as you have said before on other occasions, it really isn't any of your business, except that I don't mind telling you. I was engaged last year. It didn't take. I guess it was by mutual consent, partly because my heart was so set on making this trip. Perhaps I haven't yet seen the man that I'd feel like spending the rest of my life with."

He shot her a sly look. "I must say, though, you and your friend Graham seemed to be hitting it off pretty well last night up there on deck."

That scene with its unexpected kiss and embrace! Why must he bring that up to spoil things? "No reason why we shouldn't be 'hitting it off pretty well,' as you put it, is there?" she asked icily.

He grinned. "Just checking on progress."

"You seem to be doing all right, too," she said, then could have bitten her tongue, the remark had come out sounding shrewish and almost jealous. She was angry at herself, but he seemed unconcerned at her words or her tone.

"By that, you mean my friend Dianne. I want to assure you that there is no gossip about the two of us. She and I manage to keep ourselves out of the public eye and attention. I suggest you and Graham do the same."

She turned over in her mind various responses to make, then decided to make none. One thing Wynne said was true, except for that first morning out on the pool terrace, she hadn't seen Dianne in his company, except in a group, never the two alone.

The silence between them grew long, but he didn't seem to notice; he strolled along, whistling softly under his breath, seemingly oblivious to any problems.

A sudden thought popped into her mind. "Wynne, you said you noticed on my passport that I came from Arizona. It never occurred to me before. What must the purser have thought, you living in one state and I in another? Or did he notice, do you suppose?"

"Oh, he certainly did. And asked me about it. But I told him that was all part of the emancipated-woman phase you were going through. That you insisted we lead our own lives, getting together only occasionally, a form of open marriage." He glanced down sideways at her. "I think he feels sorry for me."

"No doubt!" She could picture it, the purser exchanging a man-to-man look of sympathy with the incorrigible man by her side.

The faint sounds of music began drifting from the lounge, and Wynne touched his hand to her elbow. "Maybe we had better go locate the Babcocks and the two girls; it's about time."

The Babcocks had already secured a table next to the dance floor, Joan sitting with them. Dianne was not to be seen. Maybe, a faint hopeful thought flitted through Amanda's mind, maybe Dianne wouldn't arrive. There was something about the girl that Amanda didn't like or trust. And not, she informed herself sternly, just because of Wynne.

But luck was not with her this evening. "Wow!" gasped Joan under her breath, nudging Amanda. "Look what's coming in the door!"

Amanda turned her head to see Dianne making her way between tables to cross the dance floor toward them. One doesn't ordinarily dress formally the first night out of a port, but Dianne had chosen to do just that. A green satin gown draped closely about the voluptuous figure and the neckline was a deep revealing cleavage. Lee Babcock gave a soft low whistle. Nor was he the only one staring at the girl. Her passage across the dance floor turned one masculine head after another, following her with appraising eyes.

Lee and Wynne both rose politely as she joined them. She seated herself with a gracious smile, bending forward, precariously exposing even more cleavage.

There was a strange little moment of electric silence, then everyone began speaking at once, the sort of chatter that springs up to cover an awkward moment.

As the music began, Wynne rose to stand beside

Amanda. He didn't speak, but just put his hand gently on her shoulder. She glanced up, then rose to move over to the dance floor with him. His hands touched her lightly, but she was ridiculously conscious of them through the thin material of her pink dress.

They did not dance well together. Perhaps it was because Amanda held herself stiffly, feeling an unfamiliar shortness of breath, a thudding of heart. She was not intentionally rigid, but she could not relax in the intimacy of his hold. Even her eyes were averted, lashes swept downward as if to veil her inner emotions.

If he thought her without grace, he made no mention of it, but dutifully finished the dance, right to the end of the final encore of the number. Then he led her back to the table, her knees awkward beneath her. Stubbornly she refused to acknowledge the reason.

How strange it was that all her gracelessness vanished as she and Lee Babcock swooped around the dance floor when they exchanged dances.

Then Lee asked a rosy-faced Joan to dance and Wynne turned to Dianne, who held out her hand to him, rose, and moved to the floor, where she seemed to melt in his arms. Amanda did not want to watch as the two, and for her there were only two, dancers swirled about to the music. Yet she could not look away. What must he think of her own inept performance as he and Dianne spun gracefully about in a pattern of intricate steps? Amanda pressed her hands together in her lap, turning to Tina Babcock to give a rubbery little smile, demonstrating that she was having a good time. Which she was not.

"May we finish this dance?" Graham was suddenly there by her chair.

"Do go ahead," urged Tina. "I don't mind at all sitting here alone. I love watching."

Amanda had hesitated, but now she rose to join the dancers as Graham led her onto the floor.

"No lectures, Amanda, my love," he said softly in her ear as they moved in time to the music. "It's perfectly permissible for bachelors to politely approach even authentic wives for the pleasure of a dance." His eyes glinted wickedly. "And as for unauthentic ones . . ." His hand tightened on hers.

Cautiously edging past the troubling emotion that curled around her heart, she managed a responsive smile. What an utter, utter fool she was! Graham was the one she should be interested in. As the music came to an end, he hesitated, his arm holding her for a brief extra second before he released her and his hand moved politely to her elbow to steer her back toward her table.

He gave a token bow toward Wynne. "Thanks, Mr. Harrison. Amanda is a lovely dancer." Then he left.

Amanda didn't miss the faint quizzical lift of Wynne's eyebrow.

Somehow the evening was gotten through. Wynne led her onto the floor once more, certainly from the standpoint of appearances and duty, she realized, not from personal enthusiasm. If she performed a bit more gracefully, it was only by sheer effort, for inside she again felt taut.

After the music ended for the evening, Wynne, in a husbandlike display, escorted her to the door of the stateroom, then said, "See you later."

As she let herself into the room, she wondered if he and Dianne were having one of their late and surreptitious dates.

She was still awake but her light was out when he tiptoed into the room sometime later. She made no sound at all, trying to appear asleep. When he had settled down for the night, flicking off his bed lamp, her eyes flew open wide. Now, here in the dark, she was at last face to face with the troubling realization that had been haunting her for some time.

Her fingers scratched noiselessly on the sheet beside her rigid body. She felt miserable and disturbed. Oh, it was all very well, she reminded herself, to go on fooling herself, but it was going to do very little good. She raised her eyes as if she could pierce the dark. Up there, in that upper bunk, lay a man with whom she had fallen helplessly in love. And she had to bear his cheerful uninterested attitude. To know that if he sought romance, it was all in the direction of the girl named Dianne.

She heard him turn in bed, give a faint mumbling sigh as if he were dreaming. Amanda felt her eyes burn. She could weep with frustration. Ahead of her lay weeks of being with him and never, not once, allowing him to suspect. Weeks of sweet, bitter misery.

Chapter 6

Six days, Amanda thought, six days since we left Hawaii! Being with him hadn't grown any easier. Gazing out at the blue of the ocean, at the tiny speck of island ahead, she was grateful at least that so far he had not suspected.

But no thanks to her traitorous heart, which spun crazily whenever they brushed past each other in the narrow space between the dressing table and the bunks. Sometimes she feared he might even perceive the thudding through the thin summer clothes she wore.

But Wynne? More often than not, he was absentminded in her presence, accepting her as unavoidable complication of the trip and his job. He came, he went, speaking to her in a sort of husbandly fashion in public, scarcely more than was absolutely necessary when they were alone. He was never impolite; she almost wished he were, it would demonstrate some sign of emotion.

Would that were so about Graham! She really couldn't discourage him without being down-and-out rude. But she was cautious not to encourage him, either. Yet it mattered little; when they had a moment out of earshot of others, Graham made no secret of how he felt about her.

"I've never been so frustrated in my whole life," he had said only a half-hour ago when he had cornered her briefly in the writing room. She frowned. Life could be

98

so simple if only Graham had fallen in love with Dianne, and Wynne—if Wynne— She shrugged hopelessly. It was useless, and the sooner she got her silly emotions straightened out, the better.

The green island in the distance loomed larger and larger, verdant peaks needling up sharply above cloud-draped ravines.

"Moorea. My God, what a sight!" Wynne's voice was suddenly at her elbow.

They watched silently as the ship edged into an anchorage in the midst of a sparkling sapphire bay. Amanda could hardly breathe at the sheer beauty of land and sea.

"Treating you to lunch ashore today," he said casually. "In the line of husbandly obligation."

She started to protest, but he shook his head. "No, I don't mind. As I've said, from time to time these token demonstrations of marital bliss are necessary. Until I make some progress on my investigation, anyhow."

"And still nothing?" Amanda asked curiously.

He paused for an instant before saying, "Well, no, but sooner or later something's got to give. When it does, and I can wind it all up, I'll be off like a shot, back to the States at the first stop, and you'll have the pleasure of 224 to yourself."

Wynne grinned down at her. "Then you can say I deserted you. And poor old Graham can be free to press his romantic conquest."

"And you?"

"Oh, I've got her home address and phone number, all secured in a perfectly platonic manner, I assure you.

"Bring along your bathing suit when we go ashore," he said, turning from the railing. "Better stick in a pair of sneakers, too, if you have them. The water is great, but the coral underneath can be a problem. It can give you a nasty cut and it's often poisonous—at least cuts are pretty apt to get infected."

Amanda was ready with her beach bag as a launch pulled up alongside the ship and passengers began making their way down to the smaller boat. Mrs. Stewart was already aboard when Amanda bent to enter the small salon.

The elderly woman greeted her enthusiastically, her bright little eyes lighting up. "Ah, there you are, my dear. You will love it here on Moorea, most romantic!" She beamed up at Wynne as they moved past, but took a quick glance at Amanda's hand. "Oh, still not wearing it. That's a shame."

"What's a shame?" Wynne asked idly as they found seats in the stern of the launch.

"She thinks I ought to—to wear my wedding ring," Amanda said jerkily.

"And so you should," he said cheerfully. "That is, when you get married. Now, as for a wedding ring for men, I'm of a divided nature." He gave her an amused look. "It can be a handicap."

"I don't think it would deter your friend Dianne," she said abruptly, then wished she hadn't.

But he didn't seem to mind. "You may be right, but don't underestimate her. Or misjudge her. That girl has a lot going for her. She's not exactly dumb, whatever you think."

Their conversation was interrupted by others shoving in beside them on the long seats. The engines began churning, and the launch pulled away from the cruise ship and headed toward the incredible lushness of the small island.

Polynesians, clad in brilliant cotton prints, barefooted and with wreaths of flowers in their hair, or individual blossoms tucked over their ears, were waiting on the dock for the approaching visitors.

The hot humid air surrounded Amanda as she and Wynne stepped onshore and a fragrant lei was looped around her neck, a wreath of yellow blossoms set upon her cap of golden hair. She turned to glimpse Wynne, sheepishly grinning at her over his own necklace of frangipani.

It was a day of dreams and beauty, stolen out of the staid routine of their shipboard arrangement. For a little while Wynne seemed to drop his cool, detached manner toward her, and though he certainly was far from romantic, he was pleasantly attentive. They swam in the crystal water, fascinated by the bright-colored tropical fish that skated wildly about from under their splashing.

As they lay onshore, feeling the hot sand of the beach warming them, Wynne and Amanda watched the Polynesian dancers swaying sensuously to the music of stringed instruments.

"Now I know what is meant by a tropical paradise," Amanda murmured happily. "No wonder my parents wanted so badly to return." For a moment the scenery dissolved into a mirage where her mother and father, young and happy, walked hand in hand along the palm-fringed shore.

"You are a very sentimental young woman, aren't you, Amanda?" Wynne said gently, then his tone changed. "And, I must admit, a very stubborn one. With a temper as quick as that of an angry mongoose."

She turned to him. "I've never heard of a mongoose having a bad temper, or a good one, either. Are you an expert on mongooses, or mongeese?" she asked idly, running her hand through the sand.

"Naturally. But I happen to be just as expert in the field of tropical sun. Just a few more moments out here and that shell-pink skin of yours is going to turn lobster red." He touched a testing finger to her bare shoulder. "Medium well already."

Her warm skin tingled where he had touched her, but she scrambled to her feet, clasping her beach bag and towel. Wynne followed her up into the shade, but held out a quick hand to stop her.

"Wait, be careful, look up above." He had pulled her slightly aside, so she was not directly under the tall coconut palm.

She lifted her head to stare up at the spreading green fronds where, nestled close to the center, clustered masses of green husked coconuts, large as footballs.

"It's only this past year that Tahiti has had more death from auto accidents than from falling coconuts," he warned her. "There aren't as many cars here on Moorea, so maybe the old ratio still is good. Anyhow, be careful. Let's take some chairs over there under one that's a little less lethal."

They settled into beach chairs under an umbrella-shaped tree, but Amanda was still twisting her head to gaze back at the coconut palms. "It's fantastic to think that something you see every day in the supermarket back home could turn out to be so dangerous here."

"It is, though, so watch where you walk." He held up his hand to signal a Polynesian waitress who had wandered out of the open-air, thatched hotel nearby. In moments the girl returned with plates of fresh pineapple, papaya, and mango.

Wynne watched with amusement as Amanda ate her way happily through the moist, delicious fruit. "I must say, I'm just as glad our marriage is of the counterfeit type. I'd hate to pay your grocery bills."

"But it is so good!"

She was not quite as enthusiastic when the girl brought strange-looking dishes to place on the table beside them. But Amanda was willing to try, and she nibbled tentatively at a small cubed vegetable, then lifted her eyes. "I'm not so sure about this. Tastes a little like"—she took another small bite—"like a mealy potato."

"Breadfruit." He pointed to a deeply green-leaved tree a few feet from them where large pebbled balls hung.

She pushed the plate a bit away, trying, in turn, plantain, which she thought tasted like weary sweet potatoes, then a delicate and delicious morsel of fish.

"This I like," she pronounced positively.

His eyes glinted, mouth twitching. "Raw fish."

She glanced up at him, back at her plate, then stubbornly took another bite. "I like it," she said, though not as positively.

The rhythmic rumble of native drums began reverberating across the beaches and through the hotel grounds as a group of Polynesian dancers started gathering in a circle not far from Wynne and Amanda, their golden brown bodies gleaming in the hot sunlight. The women, in swaying grass skirts and flower-covered halters, and the men, in brilliant red, short, wrapped *pareus,* all wearing frangipani crowns and ginger leis about their necks, began the graceful sensuous undulations of the Polynesian dance.

Amanda watched, entranced by the unaffected charm and beauty of the performers. For a little while she was caught up in the magical spell of the lush tropical isle, the scent of fragrant blooms, the rhythm of the throbbing music.

It was almost a shock when the dancing ended, the dancers drifted away, and Amanda found herself suddenly returned to reality. Graham's eyes caught hers for a moment as she glanced around. Sitting at the table with him was Harry Shields, the inevitable cigar in his mouth, his bright parrot-patterned shirt clinging wetly to his thick shoulders. Poor Graham, she thought; what a trial it must be to have that coarse vulgar man sharing a room. No doubt the man had attached himself to Graham for the day's outing.

Amanda brought her attention back to Wynne, who was beginning to gather up towels and his sunglasses. "It's about time," he said, smiling at Amanda and holding out his hand to help her to her feet. "I hate to break this up, but pretty soon the launch is going to be getting ready to deliver us back to the ship. Maybe we'd better change clothes so we'll be ready. If we have any spare time, then we can stroll around the area."

They parted, Wynne to the men's dressing room to the left of the sprawling hotel complex, Amanda crossing through the open-air lounge to go around to the right. On her way her ear was caught by Mrs. Hildebrand's strident voice. "Heathens! That's what they are! I thought we sent missionaries to make Christians out of them. Did you see that dance, Claude? Indecent, that's what it was, wiggling their hips like—like wicked women."

If Claude summoned up courage to do anything but agree, Amanda never found out, for she was already out of hearing. She walked into the dressing room to change out of her bathing suit. Funny, she thought, he had simply touched her shoulder, just once, lightly, yet sensation still lingered. She looked into the mirror, her skin was undoubtedly slightly sunburned, but she almost expected to find a small light circle where his finger had been for so brief a moment.

She stood there, torn between two emotions, troubling love and straight-out anger. She was affected by him, no doubt about that, she admitted; he aroused a strange and tremulous feeling inside her. But she was furious at herself. This silly schoolgirl infatuation, all right then, call it love, she thought rebelliously, whatever it was, it was useless. He'd made clear that she wasn't his type. And the redhead . . . just as clearly the kind that was.

Amanda gritted her teeth, her eyes glaring at the reflection in the glass. All she needed was a little more willpower. He wasn't the only man in the world. Where was her pride? After a stern lecture delivered to the girl in the mirror, Amanda began to dress rapidly. Wynne would surely be waiting, perhaps impatiently, for she had been wasting time. Not really wasting, she reflected, she had come to a firm decision to fall completely out of love with him.

He was not outside where they had agreed to meet. She stood, gazing around, but there was no sign of him. Somewhat away, over to her left, there was a knot of people, some of them passengers from the ship. Perhaps they were getting ready to board. After a quick look around once again, Amanda went over to the group. But they were not preparing to leave; they were in a circle, bending over something on the ground and murmuring.

Protruding from the spectators, a pair of woven sandals were sprawled on the close-matted grass. Amanda gave an involuntary cry as she recognized the shoes. *Wynne!* Pushing ruthlessly through the group, she stared down at the unconscious man on the ground, one of the passengers bending over him.

"It's his wife, let her through," a voice said. "That's your husband, he got hit by a falling coconut."

The man attending Wynne looked up to meet her eyes. "He's lucky, not hurt badly as far as I can tell, knocked out for the moment, though." He returned his attention to Wynne.

Amanda felt seized by a strange immobilizing paralysis. Then, slowly, almost automatically, she sank to her knees beside the injured Wynne. How pale he looked. How vulnerable. Her heart twisted painfully.

"He—he's going to be all right?" she beseeched the person attending Wynne, her face drawn with anxiety.

"I'm pretty sure. I'm a doctor, but we better have the

ship's physician look him over when we get on board, just to be certain, you understand. See, he's beginning to stir now."

Wynne's tangled black lashes fluttered slightly and the color started coming back into his face slowly, but he still lay inert.

"God, it's dangerous to walk under these damned trees," someone in the rear of the group was saying. "Everyone ought to be warned when they come ashore."

But Wynne knew! Amanda let her gaze travel slowly to where a large green coconut sprawled nearby, then looked back at Wynne. Why had he ignored his own instructions? She lifted her head to concentrate her eyes on the tree that had caused the accident. Strangely, it was not directly above Wynne, but a little to one side. Maybe he had cut across under the branches, the fanlike fronds, but far enough from the dangerous objects so as to feel perfectly safe. Had a stray gust of wind sent one of them plummeting down on his head?

Suddenly his eyes opened, blinked once or twice, then widened as he tried to struggle unsteadily to a sitting position.

"Here, take it easy," cautioned the doctor. "Don't try to get up yet."

Wynne lifted his hand to feel gingerly at the side of his head. "What happened?" he asked painfully.

"You got hit by a falling coconut," the medical man replied.

"The hell I did!" Wynne blurted. "How could I? I wasn't under a tree."

The man shrugged. "Well, that's what happened. We found you stretched out and the coconut a foot or two away. That's all it could have been. And you've got a knot on the side of your head from the impact. You're a pretty lucky guy, you know. Could have been a lot worse."

Wynne's eyes moved around the group to fasten suddenly on Amanda, kneeling beside him. "I didn't see you. Don't worry, I'm okay." He shook his head as if to clear his thoughts, then his face twisted painfully. "That hurts," he muttered.

After a moment he got unsteadily to his feet, helped by the doctor. Wynne swayed dizzily, then took a deep breath, clearly making an effort to pull himself together.

Amanda rose, too, brushing bits of grass from her knees, her face still anxious. "Wouldn't you like to go somewhere and sit down until we leave for the ship?" she asked.

He turned to look at her with a strange expression, as if he had completely forgotten about her. Then his eyes blinked once or twice before he spoke, "Sit? Ah, yes, maybe I'd better."

Walking without help now, if still a bit unsteadily, he sat gingerly on the edge of a chair, as if fearing to move his head by sudden motion. For a few moments the doctor stood by, as if to be certain all was well with his unexpected accident victim. Then, seemingly assured, he rejoined his own group of friends.

Amanda took a chair next to Wynne. "May I get you something? Do you want a cold drink? Anything?" she asked helplessly. She had to restrain herself from reaching out to touch that crisp dark hair, worriedly, lovingly. The temptation was so real that she quickly locked her hands together in her lap.

"No, nothing," he answered absently, eyes narrowed, mouth pulled to a straight hard line. "Let me think a few minutes. I've got something to sort out in my mind." He fell silent.

After several moments of silence he got to his feet, steady enough now, and looked down at Amanda. "I'm all right. My head hurts like hell, but the dizziness is gone. I've got to go take a look."

Without waiting for her to protest that he might better continue to rest, he was cutting across the green, matted grass to where the coconut still lay. Amanda followed. He stood, hands on hips, glancing up at the nearby tree, then back at the sizable object on the ground.

A wry grin, whose humor did not reach his eyes, twisted his mouth. "So I'm getting close. I wish I knew positively to whom. And what this little trick was supposed to accomplish, unless"—his face darkened—"unless it was to finish me off or put me out of commission for the rest of the trip. That's all it could be."

Amanda felt her nerves recoil in sudden shock. "You mean it wasn't accidental? That someone . . . ?" She halted, gazing up at the tree. "But how, Wynne, how could they climb clear up there? It's so terribly high, there are no limbs to pull up with." She shook her head. "Wynne, I don't think—"

He brushed aside her words impatiently. "Not from the tree, I tell you. I wasn't where I could have been hit by anything falling. But thrown? That's something else. Take a look around you at the hotel cottages, the thatch-roofed huts where people stay. See how they're raised off the ground on stilts? Someone could, probably did, sneak into an empty one and hope I'd pass close enough on my way back from changing. There's enough height from one of the windows to give a coconut momentum if the occupant tossed it hard."

His hand seemed to unconsciously lift to touch his head where he'd been hit. "The blow didn't come from the top, but on the side, which ought to prove what I'm saying. I think that someone, whoever it was, took a quick look to be sure no one was looking and—God what a chance he took—to quickly drag me close to one of these trees. It's only a matter of a foot or so."

Wynne twisted. "Take a look at my back. See any signs of dragging?"

Amanda's startled eyes could easily trace the staining of his sport shirt with the green of the turf, splotches of dirt, a few small leaves. "Yes, I—I guess you're right, Wynne. It's there."

"Okay then, forget it. Just put the whole thing out of your mind," he said bluntly, but not unkindly. "You've got worry lines. I'm all right. I'm going to be all right. You are not concerned in this; it's strictly between me and"—a contemplative frown angled his dark eyebrows—"and whoever is anxious to get me off his trail."

Amanda found no words with which to reply as she struggled with the implications, the terrifying implications of what he was saying. That someone had been in the stateroom, going through her dresser drawers, had its own little aura of fear, making her a little nervy, but not like this. She stared at Wynne, her heart driving against her ribs in sickening jerks as full realization finally flooded over her, leaving her shaken. Someone might have killed him. And, if part of his guess was right, someone fully intended to.

She looked about her as the other passengers began to gather together, preparing to board the launch. Someone from the ship. It had to be.

"Wynne, you've got to be careful, but what can you do if you don't know who it is?" She turned back to gaze at him, her voice thin and shaking, very unlike her own.

"I told you not to worry, Amanda. I mean it. Threat is an occupational hazard in my line of work, so is the attempt at mayhem—or more." He looked remote, absorbed, and the slightest bit impatient.

There was no reply to make to that, so she made none. But, nevertheless, she could not obey his order not to worry. Every glimpse of the stains on the back of his shirt, the way he carried his obviously aching head, increased, not lessened the anxiety.

"Looks like we'd better join the crowd; they're beginning to board," Wynne said, brushing sketchily at the back of his shirt, knocking off the bits of leaves and grass.

Wordlessly she turned to go with him, down the curving walk to the dock, her eyes unconsciously searching the crowd ahead of them, almost as if she thought that she might instinctively be able to guess who had attacked Wynne.

"Say, Wynne, what happened to you?" Lee Babcock's voice broke into her intent watching. "We were on the other side of the hotel, along the far beach. Just heard you got hurt."

"Yeah, a coconut," Wynne answered.

"Hey, that's dangerous!" Lee's tone rose sharply. "Hear that, Tina?" He turned to his wife. "See why I told you to watch out?" Back to Wynne, squinting appraisingly, he said, "You going to be okay? Look a little pale."

Wynne stepped over the railing of the launch, holding out his hand to aid Amanda. "Sure, left me with a headache, but I've had worse ones with a hangover," he replied smoothly. Only the tightness of his mouth told Amanda that the light touch was all on the surface.

Other passengers murmured their inquiries and concern as they went by, some few eyeing him with open curiosity, a morbid interest in their faces.

When they reached the cruise ship, Amanda suggested that Wynne lie down for a while after he'd seen the doctor. But he brushed off the latter suggestion. "I'll lie down for an hour, try some cold packs on my head, just on general principles, but I mean it when I say I'm okay now. I don't need a doctor to tell me so."

So Amanda left him the stateroom to himself and went up on deck.

She needed to be alone for a while, do a little thinking about what had occurred, feeling no desire to engage in casual shipboard chitchat with anyone at present. Making her way to the uppermost deck, where few strollers strayed, she stood at the railing to look down at the water and the preparations for sailing on to Tahiti.

Yet she saw nothing but her own troubled thoughts, her concern about Wynne. Bitterly she reminded herself that she didn't even have the right to the emotional reaction she had and was still having. Even the red-haired girl could unknowingly claim more of a right than she, if amorous interest meant anything.

The sound of footsteps behind her broke into her thoughts, and before she could turn, the odious reek of stale cigars greeted her.

Harry Shields, small sharp eyes searching her face candidly, reached up to take the cigar slowly from the corner of his mouth. "Hear the mister had a little accident on the outing today. He all right now?"

Why did she find him so repugnant? Amanda controlled her inner reaction and said quietly, "Yes, thank you, he's resting."

"Someone said a coconut fell on him. For a minute I thought they were kidding. Crazy kind of thing to have happen to a guy, isn't it, when you think about it? Here you can travel thousands of miles on a trip and, bonk, you get beaned while you're on some corny little island clear out here in the Pacific Ocean." Clearly he intended to continue their conversation.

"I understand it isn't an uncommon accident in this area," she responded courteously. Suddenly she realized that one of the things that disturbed her about the man, something she hadn't thought of before, was that he didn't look like a tourist, he didn't act like a tourist. And she was at a loss to know why.

He lifted the cigar and puffed on it silently for a moment, eyes never leaving her face. Then he withdrew the cigar. "He oughta be careful. People can have all kinds of accidents when they are at sea like this, or in some of these strange foreign places." His mouth closed around the cigar once more.

Was that meant as a warning, or simply a friendly bit of advice? The heavy face did not reveal the answer. He merely nodded. "You tell him to take care." And he walked away.

Uneasily Amanda watched him go. She must warn Wynne about Harry Shields. She had mentioned her doubts about him before, but this was something more substantial. She ran her memory carefully over the words: "He oughta be careful. People can have all kinds of accidents. . . ." Wasn't there a sly undercurrent of threat?

For a long time she watched as preparations were concluded for the sailing and the big ship began pulling out again to the open sea. She strolled about on deck then, until the wind freshened and blew her hair about her face. Glancing down at her watch, she saw she had been up here more than two hours, dinnertime not far off. Perhaps she had better see how Wynne was faring, he had said he wanted to rest but an hour.

At the stateroom door, she tapped softly. There was no answer. She waited, tense. Perhaps he was worse, perhaps— She plunged her hand into her purse and drew out her key.

The room was very still and in partial gloom of early evening. Amanda shut the door quietly behind her and stood listening. She could hear nothing. Looking up, she could see the covers mounded as if someone slept beneath them, but she was unsure if there was any sound of breathing. She tiptoed to the ladder leading to the upper bunk and silently made her way up to it, hesitant but disturbed.

He was there, lying on his back, eyes closed. Leaning forward, hardly able to breathe for nerves, she bent closer and closer, making not a sound.

Suddenly there was a faint movement of his eyelashes and a hand suddenly shot out to grab her wrist tightly, as he jerked to a sitting position.

"Oh, so it's you," he snapped out sharply, still holding to her wrist. "Damn it, be careful! Don't sneak up on me that way. You could get hurt." His voice was frankly angry.

She yanked out of his grip. "Why didn't you answer my knock then? How was I to know you weren't hurt again, or something?" she said with violent helpless impatience.

"That's what woke me up, I guess. Or else it was the door opening. Some sound. But the first thing I was aware of was the door closing softly, then footsteps coming up the ladder. What did you expect—after what happened this afternoon? That I'd be likely to let someone reach over and clobber me?" He touched his head with exploratory fingers, but said nothing more.

"Wynne, I—I'm sorry. I didn't think. I was afraid that you—you—" Her voice trailed off raggedly.

"Okay, maybe you're the one who's got the apology coming, but just remember that this looks, or is beginning to look, like a game someone is playing for keeps. And I'm liable to be pretty fast in reacting to anyone creeping around if I don't know who it is. Pipe up, kid." He glanced down at his watch. "Good Lord, it's about time to eat." Then he shot her an amused grin. "I don't ordinarily go to bed completely clothed, so maybe you'd better make yourself scarce for a few moments, unless

you don't mind an only slightly more decent repetition
of the first time we met."

Amanda backed down the ladder hurriedly to the ac-
companiment of a muffled chuckle from above. At the
bottom, she asked, trying to hide the indignation in her
voice, "*Should* you be getting up? Why not have your
dinner served here?" She was glad he could not see her
face, which had reddened at his comment. And she certainly wasn't going to give him the satisfaction of knowing.

"I'm all right, except for a slight headache. If there
had been a little more height or more speed and force
behind that coconut, I might not have a headache at all,
or anything else but a fancy funeral. As it is, I'm hun-
gry."

He stirred as if to come down the ladder, so she
whirled abruptly to leave the room. He was absolutely
impossible, she decided, going down the passageway;
she wasn't certain if he had been kidding about being
unclad, or not. Indeed, the more she considered it, the
more she realized she wasn't certain of very much about
Wynne. He was like trying to put your finger down
firmly on quicksilver.

Why, she goaded her mind stubbornly, why did she
care so about him, when he had made it so painfully evident that she didn't interest him in a romantic way?

Ahead of her, down at the end of the long corridor,
Amanda caught a glimpse of Mrs. Stewart's slight figure,
her white head bent in animated conversation with another elderly woman. Amanda could almost picture Mrs.
Stewart's excited response, should she learn that the accident of today was no accident at all. But she mustn't
know, nor must anyone else. Wynne had emphasized
that he wanted his profession and mission kept a complete secret. And, so far, it seemed to be . . . with one

frightening exception: the man who had thrown the coconut.

Suddenly she halted, aghast. She had forgotten to tell Wynne of her recent encounter with Harry Shields . . . and it might well be important.

Chapter 7

Amanda waited until she felt certain that Wynne had had time, and more, to complete dressing, then she went back to knock at the door.

He opened it, comb in hand. "I've something I forgot to tell you. I'm not certain how important it is, but it may be," she explained as he stepped into the bathroom and stood before the mirror to finish combing his hair.

"Harry Shields made a comment to me a short time ago. It was not just what he said, but the way he said it, that made me wonder," Amanda continued, watching his dark hair crisp into place, the very act seeming somehow queerly intimate. Stop it, she told herself sharply, you're becoming an absolute fool!

She went on, relating Shields' words as accurately as she could. "What do you think?" she asked intently.

He turned. "Think? My first instinct would be to wonder, as you did. Maybe he's warning me off, letting me know that the incident on the island today was only a beginning, from now on things might get rougher. Or"— he hunched a shoulder as if to dismiss the thought—"or it could be a simple casual statement of concern, one anyone might make."

"But you really should be careful, Wynne."

"Look, Amanda, maybe you don't know it, but I've been careful. Today was pure fluke, a one-in-a-million possibility. But you don't get to be old in the investigating business unless you start right out expecting something to happen, because it often does. All right, now, let's talk about food. Do you want to wait until the time we are docked in Tahiti and try one of the late dinner spots in town, or shall we eat on board now?"

"Let's have dinner here," she said. "We won't be able to dock and go ashore for at least another hour or more, and I'm not sure you should go ashore tonight anyhow." She eyed him. "You still look a little pale."

He grinned. "You don't. You've got the beginnings of a glorious sunburn.".

She gave a quick glance in the mirror. Her cheeks were unusually pink and the tip of her nose glowed.

"Watch the tropical sun, as I warned you, Amanda. Arizona may be hot, but this is something else." He slipped into his jacket. "See you in the dining room in a few minutes?"

She nodded and he left. When she arrived at the door of the dining salon, he was waiting; they entered together, to be met with a wave of comments from the dinner table.

"I say, you got a proper cosh, didn't you?" queried Joan. Dianne was almost intimately solicitous in her concern. But Wynne merely smiled, told them all he felt perfectly all right. The Babcocks were planning on doing the nightlife of the port of Papeete in Tahiti and gave a blanket invitation for everyone to join them, looking hopefully at Wynne. "If you feel up to a late-night pub crawl. We can come back anytime you want to."

Wynne, after a quick glance at Amanda, begged off a decision for the moment. "We'll let you know later, if you don't mind."

But Wynne was reluctant to go ashore until the next morning.

"Amanda, I've simply got to give the room another search," he said as they strolled the deck after dinner.

"I've just decided. Tonight. After what happened today I'm more than ever certain that whatever I'm looking for is there. Otherwise, the incident on Moorea makes no sense. If we go into town tonight, then it's practically extending an uninterrupted open-house invitation to my opponent. Amanda, I know it's there! But, damn it, where is it?" He thrust his hands into his pockets angrily.

"But you've looked, you said you'd covered every possibility."

"I have. Now I'll go back and start over again, right from the beginning, and look just as if I'd never done it before. And this time I won't stop with 'every possibility.' I'll cover every impossibility." The angles of his jaw lengthened and hardened, his face all at once looked infinitely remote and withdrawn.

She hesitated to break in on this silent and isolated air of his. But after a moment or two it was he who abruptly broke the silence with a sudden switch of mood.

"Don't let me spoil any plans you want to make, however. Why not run into town with the Babcocks? They like you, and I know they'd be glad to have you along." He was even smiling now. She had the feeling he'd just as soon have her out of the way. This was the professional, clearing the way of interruptions.

Well, he needn't worry. "I may," she replied airily. "I might even ask Graham to join the party." Amanda smiled blandly.

He shot her a sharp look. "Is that wise?"

"Oh, you mean from the gossip angle? We wouldn't be together, really. He'd be one of the group. I imagine Joan and Dianne are covered in a sort of blanket invitation. Or so I gathered. Anyhow, I'm not sure, I may or I may not."

He hesitated, almost as if he wanted to say something,

then didn't, contenting himself with a brief "See you later, then."

Amanda felt the faintest touch of guilt. She had no intention of going into town with the Babcocks, but she hadn't been able to resist responding with the same jaunty air he so often displayed toward her.

Besides, she wanted to see Tahiti by daylight. Dusk had fallen and her first glimpse of Papeete, the capital, was not quite what she had expected. Where were all the green stately palms lifting above the white beaches? And where were the white beaches? The ship had anchored in the dock area, so that all she could see were copra-drying sheds, the coconuts split and drying with their strange haunting odor, then a stream of loading trucks and in the distance, the town itself, clogged with stop-and-go traffic.

Graham found her and stood with her awhile, trying to persuade her to go with him into town. "Come on, let me show you the real Tahiti. I can take you to places the average tourist won't find in a hundred years. We'll have the place to ourselves and the natives of the island." He smiled down at her, his gray eyes warm and intimate. "If the nightlife you have seen is confined to Arizona, wait until you get a look at the Polynesian version. It's noisy, uninhibited, exuberant."

"Thanks, Graham, but not tonight. You're nice to ask me but—" She hesitated, not even certain why she was refusing. There wasn't a reason in the world why she shouldn't go, if she wished to. He'd assured her they'd not run into any of their shipmates, if that were the important drawback. Still she found herself resisting, and more than a little irritated that this was so.

"Harrison's okay, isn't he? That's not why, is it? I saw him in the dining room at dinnertime."

"He's . . . yes, I think he is. He says so. But that isn't the reason. Somehow, going into town for a long evening doesn't have the ordinary appeal for me tonight. I'm sunburned." She touched her warm cheeks fleetingly. "And Moorea itself was quite an outing for one day."

He leaned forward to lay his hand gently on her cheeks, too. Then he straightened. "So you are. I knew you looked glowing, but I hoped it might be due to my presence," he teased her lightly. Then he changed the subject back to Wynne's accident. "That was a close call, I understand. He could have been badly hurt."

She nodded, the ripple of a shiver passing over her. "Too close a call, really. Luckily, it did little more than give him a king-sized headache for a couple of hours."

Graham was standing close to her, so close that his arm touched hers. How strange was emotional chemistry, she thought. When Wynne so much as brushed past her casually in their narrow stateroom, she was achingly conscious of him. She was conscious of Graham's contact, too; it wasn't unpleasant, but it simply didn't send her blood surging through her body.

Her companion gave a quick glance either way, up and down the long curving deck, then gathered her into his arms briefly, gazing down into her eyes searchingly. "Amanda, don't you realize what a damned difficult situation I find myself in? My intentions are what is known as completely honorable, but I haven't the ghost of a chance to put them into operation. What am I going to do?"

She pulled back a few inches, trying to somehow gracefully slip from his arms. Then, finally, she had to resort to gently pushing his arms away. "Please, no, Graham."

"Amanda, look at me," he insisted.

Reluctantly she lifted her eyes. "Yes, Graham?"

He studied her closely. "All right, let's clarify things. Is it because of your absurd situation? Or is the stumbling block"—he hesitated momentarily—"me?"

late droop of his mouth, the slightly tousled hair, the general look of utter frustration that he tossed her way.

"Nothing?"

"Nothing! I've gone over this room inch by inch, both before the beds were made up and after," he said shortly. "And the worst of it is I'm becoming more and more certain it's here, somewhere." He glanced almost angrily around the four walls.

"Wynne, maybe I shouldn't bring this up, but did you ever consider that what you are looking for might have been on the body of the man when he was thrown overboard, and that's where it is now, somewhere in the Pacific?" Amanda sank into the one chair the room provided.

"Sure. But it isn't. It was reported that someone had gone through everything before the ship knew the man was missing. And gone through in a hurry, for pockets in suits were turned out, drawers in a mess, contents on the floor. Maybe the searcher was afraid of being interrupted suddenly, so he must have given a fast look . . . and got out even faster." Wynne eased himself down the ladder. "Do you think, this being the case, that the dead guy's body wasn't searched before it went overboard? Of course it was!"

He was standing in front of her now, his knees almost touching hers. She was pleased to find that even if her heart stepped up its rate the slightest bit, her breathing and her expression were under control.

Amanda was puzzled. "If you can't find it, and neither has anyone else been able to, then what are you going to do?"

"Keep looking. It's here." Then he dismissed the topic. "Didn't you go into town, Amanda? If so, you're back sooner than I thought you'd be."

"I decided against it. I'm tireder than I thought."

"I guess I am, too. A near concussion doesn't do much

to rest and relax you. I'll absent myself for a few moments so you can get to bed, if you wish."

"It won't take long," she agreed.

But it was useless to try to pretend she was already asleep when he returned, so she compromised by pulling the sheet up tightly to her neck after flipping off her light. When he entered, he bent down to look at her.

"Say, you know, you look like a rabbit bedded down for the night, with that pink nose poked up over the covers." Then he laughed, straightened, and went whistling cheerfully into the bathroom, his pajamas whipped from the closet and draped over his arm.

Well, that was a romantic comment, she thought ruefully, reaching up a finger to touch the tip of her nose. Then she went quickly back over her thoughts to firmly cross off the word "romantic." She was not even going to think the word in any connection with Wynne.

When he had crawled up the ladder and into his bunk, he switched off his own light. After a few moments of noisily plumping his pillow, sighing, and yawning, he said drowsily, "You know, Amanda, I'm getting so used to having you around as a bedroom companion that I'm actually going to miss it when my trip's over."

"And that's when you find the thing?" she asked tightly, knowing the discovery would mean the end of any chance of seeing Wynne again. New York was a long distance from Arizona. And though a thoroughgoing romance might make the trip across most of the country worthwhile, she knew he wasn't about to do it for another chance to see her.

"Yep. Then I'll take off." He yawned. "G'night," he murmured, already sounding half-asleep. In moments his steady breathing told her he was now wholly asleep.

And just like that! While she lay awake every night for some little time, knowing he was up there, where, if she really wanted to, she could almost touch him. And yet she was separated from him by more than distance. Turning over firmly on her side, she bunched her pillow under her head and clenched her eyes shut, tightly, until at last she fell asleep.

Next morning, he poked his head out the bathroom door to call over to her. "Say, thought it'd be a good idea to take in Papeete and environs today. Want to go along?" His voice was completely casual, as if he didn't care either way.

"Why, yes, I—I guess so." It was only with effort that she managed to match his careless tone.

"Okay then, as soon as I vacate the place, how about putting on a little steam and skip any long beautifying process? We'll head for out of town somewhere, into the boondocks where we can catch a glimpse of the real Tahiti. Besides, Amanda"—he grinned at her—"you don't have to go to any effort for me, I've seen how you look in the morning."

Oh, great! That was just the kind of remark that sets a girl up for the day! She looked indignantly at the bathroom door that had closed quickly after his comment.

Wynne had rented a car and it was waiting for them at the foot of the gangway as they descended. He drove easily, maneuvering the car expertly around the crates and boxes that crowded the dock, waiting to be loaded onto the ship. The air was hot and humid, heavy with the smell of copra. Amanda looked at the copra sheds as they passed, the coconuts chopped in half, their white inner meat pulling away from the husks as it dried under the blazing sun.

"What do they use copra for?" she asked curiously, wrinkling her nose slightly at the strongly pungent smell.

"Coconut oil and a lot of other things, I guess. From what I hear, it's a pretty important export," he said, whipping the car out of the way of a speeding motorist who had suicidally raced across an intersection. "Whew," he muttered, "some of these guys drive like they've gone mad."

Traffic snarled and thickened as they entered the business section, which curved along the waterfront. Myriads of yachts nestled thickly together along the shoreline.

Amanda's eyes strained to take in everything. "It's not at all what I expected," she said, dazed. "You'd think you were in a city back home at rush hour. And all the shops and traffic lights!"

He grinned, not taking his eyes off the tangle of cars jockeying for a space to dart into. Pedestrians at the intersections chattered in a rapid staccato that Amanda realized was French, their words picked up and lost as the light changed and Wynne drove on.

Before long, the traffic lessened, becoming almost sparse as Wynne left the city far behind them. On one side, the ocean stretched out in an unending sparkling azure, rolling lazily up on the long curve of shoreline. On the other side of the road, green masses of coconut palms, breadfruit trees with their queer dangling pebbled balls, and thick stalky banana plants with their shiny long broad leaves screened all behind them like verdant walls.

Amanda relaxed back against the car seat, feeling it warm against her shoulders. This, she thought, was the first time they had ventured anywhere alone. Moorea didn't count, for half the ship had come ashore and were all around them. Here, she and Wynne were by themselves. She moved her head slowly, letting her eyes slide his way. The strong profile, the ridiculous long tangled eyelashes caused her to look away quickly. If this was the way she planned to discipline her emotions, she reflected guiltily, she was doing a miserable job of it.

She tried distracting herself with a question. "Wynne, what if you fail to find whatever you are looking for? What will you do?"

"I'll find it," he spoke sharply. "It's there!"

"But what about leaving the room for today? Won't that give your opponent, as you call him, a chance to slip inside and look?"

"Last night, I'd have said so. I thought so. But if I haven't found it with all my looking, and I've done a lot of it, then I don't see how a hurriedly searching guy, who's got to feel nervous about being caught in someone else's room, is going to locate it so easily. The whole thing is going to turn out to be a matter of my continuing to search, over and over."

"But," she said suddenly, "what about the thief? Isn't catching him important, too? And if you think he's on board . . . ?"

He turned the car from the road and down a sanded path toward a sprawling, thatch-roofed building near the beach. "On board?" he said, almost as an absent afterthought. "Yeah, I'd say he is, that's what I've been going on. But my job is to recover the jewels. If I turn up the crook, that's fine, too."

They drew up in front of the open-air structure that Amanda could now see was a beach hotel. A pretty dark-skinned Polynesian girl with a bright flower tucked over her ear met them at the door and showed them to a table that looked out at the sea.

The rest of the day passed in a rosy cloud for Amanda. They walked along the shore, picking up shells; they got in their car again, driving lazily along back roads where giggling, scantily clothed children waved to them, their smooth brown skins shining in the sunlight as they darted in and out of the thickly wooded areas.

And Wynne? He was pleasant, instructive about the

countryside, and just about as romantic as a stone. She might as well be his maiden aunt whom he was politely showing the sights.

"When the trip's over, what are your plans?" he asked idly. "Going back to Arizona for good?"

"Yes," she said, trying to keep her voice from sounding dispirited.

"You sure?" He slanted a quick sideways glance at her. "How about your friend Graham, if I'm not being too curious? You know, I somehow get the feeling he'd like me to get out of the picture, leave the ship, so he could have the field to himself."

"Well, he has mentioned something like that."

"I just bet he has. You know, Amanda, our unfortunate mix-up in housing hasn't been the greatest thing for personal romances, has it?"

She couldn't resist saying, "You are speaking from your own experience, I gather."

"Yep. In a way." He had turned the car and was now starting back toward town and the end of the day. "But it has its advantages, too. Keeps one from getting in deeper than desired. I don't know about you, but I've got more on my mind than marriage right now—or, as one might put it, a meaningful love affair. Shipboard romances are noted for being sudden, emotional, and short-lived. A little modest flirtation is as far as I plan to go."

Amanda wasn't sure if she felt relieved that at least he wasn't irrevocably enamored of the red-haired girl, or if his statement sounded the death knell for any small forlorn hopes she might have. Not, she cautioned herself, that she'd really had any, he'd calmly said she wasn't his type.

When they returned to the ship, Amanda thanked Wynne for the day's outing. She nodded her head at the city with its bustling traffic. "Papeete may be part of Tahiti, too, but I'm glad I had the chance to see the Tahiti that Gauguin painted and my parents used to talk about."

The heavy aroma of copra floated on the still warm air as they walked up the gangway to enter the air-conditioned atmosphere inside the ship.

"You go ahead to the stateroom if you want to," he said. "I'd like to see about sending a message to my boss. Check in with him, but not with the news he'd like, I'm afraid." He sighed. "He isn't going to be pleased, I can tell you that. For that matter, neither am I."

With that, they parted, Wynne to go striding down one of the passageways, Amanda, the other.

Few passengers were about, and the long hallway seemed abnormally lonely and still without the sound of voices and the opening and closing of doors.

Outside her own room, Amanda took out her key and opened the door. Once inside, she stopped, her head suddenly lifting.

She recognized it at once. The smell of stale cigar smoke permeated the small room. Slowly she turned to face her closed stateroom door. Across the hall was Harry Shields, and sometime today, while they had been ashore, he had been in this room.

Chapter 8

A slow chill began curling up her spine. Warily she turned back around, throat gone dry as cardboard. The odor of tobacco was still so strong ... had she unexpectedly interrupted him?

Her eyes sought the bathroom door. It was open. She could see no one inside. Twisting her head, craning, she peered nervously, but only the bare cream-colored tiles met her eyes. The shower curtain was pulled aside; no one was there, either.

She stood, uncertain, in the middle of the room. Should she rush out to find Wynne? Somehow she didn't want to. He would certainly be returning shortly, to shower and dress for dinner. If she went out searching for him, the ship was large and she might not find him for some time. No, she decided, her heart bumping unpleasantly, she'd wait.

Cautiously she pulled out one of her dresser drawers to see if there was any indication that someone had been going through it. Everything appeared in place. One after another, she opened a drawer, gazed down, closed it. Nothing. As far as she could tell, all was as she had left it.

Drawn by something she could not understand, she went quietly over to the door, unlocked it, to peer out gingerly up and down the hall, then brought her eyes back to stare at the stateroom across from her. What she expected to see, to learn, she could not have said. Then Amanda closed her own door once again and leaned against it, tensely awaiting Wynne's arrival.

She felt a sense of relief when at last she heard footsteps coming down the hall to pause outside 224. A knock.

"Wynne?" she called, startled to find her voice thin and wavering.

"Who were you expecting?" came the cheerful reply.

She opened the door to let him in and stood back so he could get past her.

"Am I supposed to have a secret password now, roomie?" he asked; then, catching a glimpse of her troubled eyes in the mirror, he turned to face her.

"What's the problem?" he inquired, his voice gone suddenly flat and toneless.

"He's been here. While we were gone."

"Who's been here? What are you talking about?" Wynne's eyes narrowed as he searched her face.

"Harry Shields. The man across the hall." She lifted her head, catching again the faint acrid odor. "Can't you smell it—his cigar?"

Wynne tilted his head back, took a slow testing breath, then let it out in a gust that sounded almost like an exclamation.

"Well, what do you know? He isn't giving up, either." He gave a quick look around. "See any signs, anything missing? Disturbed?"

She shook her head. "Not that I know of. Not any of my things." All at once she began to tighten up inside. Her nerves bunched, and abruptly she was conscious of a heavy thudding in her chest. Her eyes were drawn to the place in the carpet where a faint difference in color indicated that a stain had once been there. Her fingers tightened at her side, as realization began to unfold inside her mind.

Someone had been murdered in this room. For something that Wynne was so certain was still here. What if—what if something could happen to her, to Wynne, simply because they were in here?

She put out a hand to clutch his arm in a quavering grasp. "Wynne," she whispered nervously, "what if he comes back? Not now, but later, when one of us is here alone?"

He patted her hand reassuringly. "Don't worry about that. He doesn't want problems. He just wants what was hidden here. That first killing had to be partly revenge on the guy for running out on his pals. So put it out of your mind. I'm not soft-soaping you, Amanda; that's the truth, you don't need to worry."

"But on Moorea you . . ."

He shook his head. "Someone's gotten wise to me, figures I'm getting too close for comfort. But you . . . forget it, kid, you are in no danger."

Wynne casually disengaged his arm, turning toward his closet to give it a quick search.

"Wynne," she said to his back, "are you close?" But of course he was, it could only be Harry Shields.

He nodded absently. "Sure. Close to who it is, but not to where it is. And that's the difference. I'm an investigator, not a policeman, just as I told you before. The police have their own methods, their own problems. Remember, I'm after a thing, not necessarily a person."

"But if you know it's Harry Shields, then can't you somehow get word to the authorities, have him arrested, at least tell the ship's officers?"

The look he gave her bordered on exasperation. "And if it isn't Shields? What if our room steward has a liking for cigars? Let me play it my way, Amanda."

Amanda knew she was being mulish, but she persisted. "You said you were getting close, which I took to mean you are fairly sure who it is."

"Maybe," he said blandly. "Now, can we begin to think about dinner?"

His run-along-little-girl-don't-bother-the-grown-ups attitude irritated her, but there was little she could do about it.

"I'll toss you for the first shower," he said, drawing a coin from his pocket.

"Heads," she said curtly.

He tossed it, glanced down, then grinned at her. "Heads it is! Want me to hold the soap?"

"Oh, very, very funny." She brushed past him, deliberately picking up her change of clothing, and headed for the bathroom, aware of his amused eyes on her back.

Why, she wondered, as the shower sprayed over her shoulders, did she let him rile her so easily? Ordinarily teasing didn't bother her in the least. And so how did she react to Wynne? With ruffled feathers and the inability to come up with any reply more novel or varied than a trite "very funny." She soaped her arms, then a smile reluctantly crept across her lips. It *was* funny, come to think of it. What she should have replied was "Please do!" That would have startled him. Right there she halted, quickly reining her thoughts, which threatened to venture into all kinds of forbidden territory. Instead, she turned the shower on harder and began soaping vigorously.

The Babcocks had not returned from shopping by the time the others had gathered around the table in the dining salon. Amanda noticed that Joan was becoming increasingly spirited as her homeland was growing closer. The girl's ruddy-cheeked face glowed.

"Oh, it's time to be getting home. I've been away for six months. Everything has been wonderful!" Joan's eyes were bright. "I liked Tahiti today, but all the time I kept telling myself, 'One more stop, in New Zealand, then the next sight will be good old Sydney Harbor and our great crouching shell of an opera house that everyone loves or hates.'" She beamed happily at them.

Dianne smiled back politely, tossed a few casual comments to Amanda, then turned to Wynne, devoting most of her attention to him.

Joan slid a quick glance at Dianne, then turned to lift her eyebrows at Amanda. "That doesn't bother you?" she asked in a low voice, her plain friendly face concerned. "Don't you mind?"

Amanda forced a reassuring smile and shook her head.

At that moment Mrs. Hildebrand, followed by her meek husband, flounced haughtily past their table, wearing an incredible muumuu of splashy orange and purple flowers.

Grateful for the interruption, Amanda whispered to Joan, "Mrs. Hildebrand has been out shopping."

Joan grinned. "She looks like sixpence of God-help-us, if you ask me."

As they were finishing coffee, the Babcocks came in belatedly, displaying their purchases of shell jewelry and small flacons of French perfume.

"Don't ask me to do any dancing tonight," Lee Babcock moaned. "My feet are worn to the ankles traipsing in and out of stores, watching my good wife boosting the local economy while depleting my wallet."

His wife tossed him a smug look. "And wools in New Zealand, opals in Australia, to begin with. I'll think of more."

Wynne leaned back in his chair lazily. "You don't have her trained, Babcock. I bought Amanda a lunch, a whirl around the island, and didn't let her near a store. You'll learn."

"Yes, but by the time I get her disciplined that well, I'll be in bankruptcy. How long have you two been married?" Lee asked.

It was as well that Wynne came up with an answer, for

Amanda opened her mouth, then shut it without a sound.

"Amanda and I," Wynne was saying, "aren't exactly newlyweds, and as you know, she's pretty liberated, so I never know whether to include the time we haven't been together. We've had our own individual lives, but I'd say it is working out in a pretty satisfactory fashion, wouldn't you say so, Amanda, dear?" He smiled at her fondly.

How adroit and yet subtly evasive his answer had been, Amanda recognized, but she nodded in agreement and added wickedly, "Yes, darling."

She had trouble restraining a triumphant grin as she saw his eyes give a startled flicker that was gone as quickly as it had appeared. It was a game two could play.

After dinner, she wasn't surprised to find Graham looking for her, finally cornering her on deck. She hadn't seen him all day and he usually managed at least a little time with her.

It was a faintly grim Graham. "Amanda, this is going to have to stop. The trip is half over and still this ridiculous charade goes on. Your friend Wynne, nice guy he may be, but he is having the best of two worlds. He has you for his pseudo-wife, and he's romancing that red-haired girl every chance he gets. We'll be in New Zealand in a matter of days; don't go on handicapping your whole trip. In New Zealand he can get a flight back to the States, or catch another boat." He put his hand on hers and looked down into her eyes. "Go to the purser and 'fess up. You were talked into it, but you can talk yourself out of it. I promise you we'll have a wonderful time, I'll show you everything onshore every place we land."

She was about to answer, not quite certain in her mind just what to say, when the soft wind blowing in from the sea caught and carried along the scent of ciga

smoke. Abruptly she jerked and twisted around, to see
Harry Shields strolling along deck, clearly heading in
their direction. Amanda's hand tightened under Graham's, her body going involuntarily rigid. She was conscious of the responsive gripping of his hand on hers.

For once, the cigar was not in Shields' mouth, but still
in evidence, gripped tightly between two stubby fingers
as he came up to them.

"Good evening, folks," he said, his voice easy and
natural. "Nice night, isn't it?" The small eyes were hard
and shiny as pebbles at the bottom of a pool.

"Hello, Shields, we were enjoying the night air and
waiting for the anchor to lift anytime now," Graham replied, rescuing Amanda from having to answer until she
was able to swallow past the sudden dryness of her
mouth.

The man's eyes moved toward her. "Enjoy yourself in
Tahiti, Miss Conklin? I saw you and your husband driving through downtown Papeete. I was standing on a
street corner, waiting to cross. Some madhouse, that
place, especially those side streets, too small with too
many cars."

Something inside Amanda hardened. If he had actually seen them, then he must have hurried back to the
ship, confident he would have uninterrupted time to
search. *If he had actually seen them—* Maybe he was lying, maybe he'd only seen them go down the gangway
and get into their car.

A desire struggled inside her to flash back at him
caustically, pinning him with the knowledge that he'd
been illegally in their stateroom. But she controlled the
urge, saying only, "Oh, I didn't see you. We drove on to
one of the beach hotels for lunch."

Shields pulled out a large handkerchief and mopped
at his face. "I guess you young folks can enjoy the night
air, as you put it, but it's still too darn hot for me. I'll be

glad when we get to New Zealand or Australia, where
it's got to be a little cooler."

"I agree, it hasn't been exactly cool today," Graham
agreed sociably.

Amanda abruptly realized that all the time they had
been talking, Harry Shields' eyes had not overlooked
Graham's hand, which still lay over hers, and that there
was an underlying appraisal in the man's regard. Instinct
made her want to quickly withdraw her hand, but she
hesitated uncertainly, wary that the action would em-
phasize the apparently more-than-casually-friendly situation.

It was with relief that Amanda welcomed the departure of the man as he said, "I'm going to check around
and see if I can't scare me up a little poker game, if
you'll excuse me. See you later, Moore. G'night, young
lady."

"Good night, Mr. Shields." Amanda was aware how
taut her voice was.

"Hope you find your game," Graham said agreeably as
the man left.

Graham waited a full two minutes before turning
slowly back to Amanda to break the silence between
them.

"All right, Amanda, what's this all about? One sight of
Shields and your hand went cold as ice. You're—well,
I'm not sure how to put it, but you act almost scared of
the man."

Amanda now withdrew her hand to brush back her
blond hair straying across her cheek, using that as an excuse. She had to answer Graham without divulging too
much. So she said simply, "He gives me the shivers,
there's something so—so furtive about him." She hoped
that would satisfy Graham.

It didn't. He looked at her intently. "There's more,

Amanda. Something is bothering you. Can't you tell me? You're afraid and that worries me."

She didn't dare. It would only reveal Wynne's undercover business on board. It wasn't her secret to disclose. So she steadied herself enough mentally to come up with an almost casual "I simply don't care for him, Graham. It's just a modern version of 'I do not love thee, Dr. Fell, the reason why I cannot tell.' "

For a moment he eyed her doubtfully, then shrugged. "Very well, Amanda. But I can't get over the feeling that your response to the man is more than spontaneous dislike."

Then he smiled down at her. "I was in Papeete today, too, and I bought a little something I want you to have." He reached into his pocket and brought out a small red velvet box.

She took it hesitatingly, then opened it. "Oh, Graham, it's lovely!" She gazed down at a small black mother-of-pearl heart dangling from a thin silver chain. Then she lifted her eyes. "You really shouldn't have bought it for me, I really—" she began, but he reached across to lightly touch her lips with two quieting fingers.

"Don't say I shouldn't. I should. I wanted to. And it's nothing expensive, only costume jewelry, made from the black mother-of-pearl shell found in local waters. Sorry, it should have been gold, or a bright-red, ruby, pulsing heart."

It wasn't what he said, but the way he said it, the tone of his voice, that faintly disturbed Amanda. It was so deeply intimate under the half-teasing surface remarks. If she were in love with him, perhaps it might be different. But, as it was, she again had the feeling that things could easily get out of hand if he felt any encouragement.

He lifted the heart out of the box. "Now, we'll have no more protests. I swear, it was this, or buy you a big purple felt pennant with a bilious green palm tree and the words 'Memory of Tahiti' stamped on it." He was fastening it around her neck. "If you don't allow me to give you this, I swear I'll rush with it to Mrs. Hildebrand and beg her to accept it as a token of my undying love."

Amanda couldn't help smiling in response. She couldn't possibly continue to refuse it, to make an issue of something he so clearly wanted her to have.

So she accepted it with thanks. "It's really lovely, Graham. But I do hate to think I'm doing poor Mrs. Hildebrand out of this beautiful little necklace."

"I shall jump ship to go back and purchase one of those pennants for her if you say so," he said, touching her gently on the cheek for only an instant, his eyes saying things his lips were not.

The ship's whistle gave a warning blast and began its slow ponderous pull away from the dock. Amanda was secretly relieved to have the moment broken between her and Graham. Other passengers strolled out of the door of the lounge to join in leaning over the railing for a last look at Tahiti, watching until the intrusive sheds and cars and buildings gradually receded, became formless, and only the green of tropical growth and white rim of beaches could be seen.

Graham still remained by her side. Someone elbowed gently in on the other side and she turned to see Wynne.

"Hello, Moore," he said shortly. Then, evidently aware his tone had sounded a bit brisk, he added, "How'd you like Tahiti?"

"Tahiti, yes; Papeete is getting too crowded and commercialized for my taste, though."

"Been here before?" Wynne leaned on one elbow.

"Yes. Done a bit of painting. Fantastic light here, makes you begin to ape Gauguin's brilliant colors unconsciously," Graham said easily, but Amanda noticed a little wariness in his eyes, as if he perhaps didn't care for competition for her attention.

Wynne was imperturbable. "An artist, are you? Always had a yen to do a little painting myself. Only one thing kept me from it: no talent." He grinned and turned back to watch the slow sweep of the water, squinting at the horizon. "Think we've got a little rain coming our way."

In moments, his words were realized as a quick tropical shower, warm and fine, suddenly drenched the open deck, sending the passengers rushing toward the doors, splattering those who lagged behind. Amanda, Wynne, and Graham, midship, farthest from the doors, sprinted, laughing and getting wet before they reached the shelter inside.

Amanda brushed back strands of hair that clung to her damp face. "It doesn't give much warning, does it? One moment a faint foggy mist in front of you, the next a downpour."

Wynne was brushing ineffectively at his shoulders, his clothing damp and limp. "Typical tropical rain. Some places have them about the same time every day, I understand. But you are right, they don't give much notice." He looked at her. "Hadn't we better go change into something dry?"

She nodded, conscious that her thin frock clung wetly to her.

"We looked like castaways with our soaked clothing," Graham said, laughing as he tried to loosen his wet shirt, which clung to his broad shoulders, as they made their way down the passageway to their rooms.

Inside 224, Amanda turned to look at Wynne questioningly.

He caught her meaning. "Look, roomie, I'm wet, I don't have any great desire to stand shivering outside the door while you indulge in a warm shower and unhurried dressing. Nor would I subject you to such barbaric treatment. So, we're adult, aren't we? Every morning we dress one *after* another. No reason why it can't be in tandem. You take the bathroom, I'll manage out here."

He made a motion toward unbuttoning his shirt, so she gave him a hurried nod, yanked open a drawer, snatched up some clothes, darted to the closet to drag a dress off the hanger, and vanished into the bathroom, breathing indignantly. She wouldn't put it past Wynne to calmly go on with his undressing until she made herself scarce.

"Now, remember to give a little warning before you open the door and come out," he called, and she heard him chuckle.

Amanda purposely did not reply. She contented herself with stripping off her clothes, the small heart dangling from its silver chain as she bent over. Graham, she thought, as she straightened up, why doesn't he arouse any response in me, at least the kind he is looking for?

She hesitated, damp clothes in hand, glancing toward the closed door. And Graham clearly resented Wynne. She sighed. Little wonder that he did. It was pretty strange to have the girl you were interested in rooming with another man.

But the same question still remained: why not Graham? For a long moment she gazed unseeingly at the wall. Then she shook her head slowly; she didn't know. There wasn't a reason why she shouldn't want to know him better, yes, even give him a certain amount of encouragement he was looking for. She only knew that she liked Graham well enough, but beyond that there was an invisible barrier that turned her back. Yes, she frowned thoughtfully, there was something about him that—that bothered her. And she had no idea what it was.

"Hey, you in there, it's awfully quiet. Gone to sleep?" A pause, then, "Want to hand me out your wet things. I'll go down the passageway to the passengers' laundry and stick them in the dryer? I'm dressed."

"No, thanks, I'll be out in a moment myself."

She dressed quickly, and when she did go into the other room, she found Wynne slouched in the chair, leaning back, legs outstretched, eyes busy with his routine preoccupation, that of studying every possible hiding place for the object he was seeking.

He brought his eyes down to look at her. Then he got to his feet slowly. Coming close to her, he lifted a finger to touch the small heart.

"I didn't notice this before. Tahitian, isn't it?" There was a question in his face.

"I didn't buy it," she explained placidly. "It was a gift. From Graham."

He still held the heart between two of his lean fingers. "Graham? Looks like things are picking up steam in that area. Between the two of you, I mean. Amanda"—he paused as if to choose his words carefully—"I always preface something I say to you with the phrase, 'Of course it's none of my business,' and it isn't, but what do you know about this Graham guy?"

Wynne sounded almost like a concerned father, she reflected with some amusement, but her next reaction was one of indignation. *He* was quizzing *her* about her romantic interests—and in that lofty manner of his— while, meantime, he was carrying on what appeared to be a red-hot romance with Dianne.

"Know about him?" she answered icily. "What do I know about you? Except what you tell me. And I'm—I'm practically living with you!"

Amanda stirred uneasily, unable to pull away because Wynne still held the necklace in his hand, but he was looking at her most queerly. How unnerving it was to see a cold stranger gazing out of a familiar face.

"Well," she said almost truculently, "I am. And I'm sure not everyone believes we are married. I really don't know much more about you than I do about Graham. For that matter, you told me at first that you were writing travel books, which you now admit you aren't. Graham says he is an artist. If I believe you, I can't see why I shouldn't believe him."

He let the heart slide out of his hands. "Very well, but just don't get in too deep before you case the situation thoroughly. You're too nice a kid to get hurt." He still had that odd look focused upon her, almost as if he were somehow trying to see into her mind.

"But you don't suspect Graham?" she wavered, the thought abruptly hitting her.

"Amanda, I suspect everyone. I have to, you know. I even had a spell, an early one, of suspecting you. But if you are asking about Graham, not especially more than I do others. For that matter, I thought you had Shields pegged as the one."

"I do. Don't you?" she asked bluntly.

"Maybe. Maybe not. All I can say is that something mighty queer is going on. And that's all I want to say at the moment." Then he gathered up his clothes. He paused as he turned back to her. Then he said, "Tell me something, are you really interested in Moore?" That strange unfamiliar look was back on his face.

What was on his mind? Amanda moistened her lips nervously. "I don't know if I am or not," she answered truthfully.

Suddenly the old Wynne was back. "Come on then, let's do our chores." With that he opened the door, bowed her out ceremoniously, and led her to the laundry. The strained moment was past.

But it came back in the dark of the night. Amanda

awakened without reason. She made several determined efforts to slip back into sleep, but perhaps the efforts were too determined, she reflected, lying with her eyes open wide now. The ship was rolling slightly, but it acted more as a comfortable cradle than anything to keep her awake.

And now the real reason came stealing back into her mind. What had caused that strange and temporary shift in Wynne's attitude—or, more precisely, in the way he looked at her? Common sense reminded her that if he didn't tell her, she had no way of knowing. Graham? Or had he changed his mind about her? Didn't he trust her? Or what?

Questions piled on top of each other until the sheer number of them acted to deaden her mind and finally she slept, a slight frown still faintly evident.

Chapter 9

The days between Tahiti and New Zealand were peaceful enough, marked only by a new and only barely noticeable restraint in Wynne. Amanda realized he still joked with her in that lightly razzing way—but less, and less spiritedly. Moreover, he was polite to her in a manner that she interpreted as coolness. But there was nothing, nothing really definite, so she gave up trying to analyze it. She recognized, however, that there had been a change in their relationship.

The ship arrived in New Zealand in early evening. At dinner the Babcocks urged Amanda and Wynne to join them in running into Auckland for a brief look around. After a quick verifying glance at Amanda, Wynne said he thought they could arrange to go. When the invitation came around the table to Joan, she agreed, but Dianne turned it down, saying blandly that she had other plans for the evening.

It was only afterward that Wynne decided not to go after all. He looked apologetically at Amanda. "I just got word from the radio room that a marine operator notified them that a call from the States is coming through to me sometime this evening, so I'd better stick around. Why don't you run along with the Babcocks?"

The Babcocks seconded his suggestion when they were approached out on deck, pressing her to join them.

They assured her it was to be a quick trip; it wasn't planned to be a night on the town. Finally Amanda agreed and hurried below to get ready.

The taxi that took them into town let them off in the business section, and the four of them strolled along, looking in windows along Queen Street.

"I can't make up my mind," said Tina Babcock. "I want some of those beautiful woodcarvings, or, no, some of those darling little Maori dolls. Oh, I know." She turned bright eyes toward her husband. "That jade ring."

He groaned, but Joan said cheerfully, "You are in luck. That's native greenstone, which I guess is a form of jade, but not as costly, I'm certain."

They wandered along, heading for no place in particular, when they came to a street crossing and Tina halted suddenly, her hand flying to cover one eye.

"What is it, Tina?" her young husband bent in concern toward his wife.

"Something . . . it blew in my eye!"

"Let me look, take your hand away," he said anxiously.

He peered into the eye that was now reddened and angry-looking. After a moment he said, "I can't see a darned thing, but it's sure red. Still hurt?"

Tina nodded, her hand once again over the eye, looking acutely uncomfortable.

"Maybe we ought to go back," Amanda said. "Let the ship's doctor work on it."

Tina halfheartedly protested, but Lee nodded. "You're right. If you two girls don't mind, maybe we'd better."

So they took a cab back to the ship, Tina and Lee heading for the doctor's office, Joan and Amanda going into the lounge.

Music was playing and a few couples were dancing.

Joan suggested the second movie show, since it wasn't terribly late.

"Thanks, not for me," Amanda said. "I saw it just before I left Arizona. But you go ahead."

Joan hesitated, then said, "If you don't mind, I think I will. I suppose you'll be wanting to join Wynne anyhow."

So they parted, and Amanda found herself heading for the stateroom almost automatically. She was nearly at the end of the passageway when she saw Dianne, slipping hurriedly around the corner leading away from stateroom 224. Instinctively Amanda pulled back into a bisecting hallway, out of sight.

The red-haired girl passed by without noticing Amanda, her footsteps slowly dying out as she went in the direction of the stairs.

Dianne's stateroom was on another deck. For a moment Amanda stood, one shoulder against the wall, her face suddenly bleak. Dianne had been in the stateroom with Wynne. No wonder he changed his plans, no doubt after talking to Dianne. She felt sick inside. But what did she expect? And what right did she have to care?

Slowly she went back into the hall and returned back the way she had come, up the steps, out onto the deck. At the railing, a short distance away, she saw Graham, standing alone, looking down at the dock, no doubt watching the stevedores loading. She turned and went quickly up to the next deck and to a far and slightly darkened corner where she could be alone.

Amanda didn't want to see anyone right now, talk to anyone. Least of all she did she want to see Wynne. Below her, on the other deck and on the dock, there were sounds of voices, onshore the rumble of trucks and buses, but she felt isolated.

The lights of Auckland blurred and she reached up to rub an infuriated hand across her eyes. What an absolute, naïve fool she had been! Bitterly she denounced herself. Just because she had this silly delusion that she was in love with that impossible Wynne Harrison, was she going to be crushed because he was intimate with Dianne?

Maybe Dianne hadn't been in their room with Wynne, maybe she had been seeing, say, Graham. She shook her head. No, Graham was up on deck and he certainly hadn't passed her in the hallway. The faint glimmer of hope died out before it even had a start.

Amanda felt morose, her heart heavy, as she stood looking out over the city. This trip was to have meant so much, to be such a sentimental occasion. "I'm sorry," she whispered, her mind on her parents now.

There were footsteps behind her and a middle-aged couple came over to the rail. "Lovely night, isn't it?" the woman asked sociably.

"Yes, it is," Amanda managed. But it wasn't, she thought drearily, it wasn't at all.

After a few moments she excused herself and left the location to the man and wife. Amanda felt tense and restless as she descended to the lower deck.

Graham was sauntering toward her, not yet aware of her, but it was too late for her to escape. She simply didn't want to talk. And now she couldn't avoid it.

"Amanda!" Graham looked surprised. "I thought you were in town. When did you come back?"

"About a half-hour ago," she answered dully.

"Funny, I didn't see you. I've been passing the time on deck, watching the activity on the dock. You see how tedious and uneventful my evenings are without you?" His quick smile was back. "What have you been doing, Amanda?" He touched her arm lightly, letting his hand remain for a moment.

"Oh, town for a while, but Tina Babcock got something in her eye, so we came back. Since then ... nothing much, just looking out at the lights." She knew her voice was a monotone, but she felt helpless to inject any spontaneity into it.

"Where's your roommate?" he asked idly. "He come back with you?"

"He didn't go." The mention of Wynne was no great help in her effort to appear casual and normal.

For a long moment Graham did not speak. It was almost a charged little silence. She was conscious that he was gazing at her in a queer searching sort of way, but she let her eyes move away and tried to think of some way to politely take her leave.

"Amanda!" He shattered the silence with an odd note in his voice. "Something is wrong. I can feel it. You are upset, Amanda. Why?"

"Wrong? Why should there be?" she evaded, without turning her head.

"Amanda, look at me. Is it something to do with"—he hesitated as if searching for a reason—"with my roommate, Shields? He's the only one I can think of who seems to affect you like this."

Now she did look at him, startled. "Harry Shields? No, that isn't it. In fact," she said limply, "it's nothing important."

Now he was persuasive, drawing her slightly closer. "You don't feel you can confide in me, Amanda, is that it?"

Before she could make a reply, they were interrupted. "Back already?" Wynne's voice cut through their conversation like a knife.

Amanda felt Graham's hand slip away from the hold he had on her arm. Getting control of herself and her voice, she answered, "Yes, about a half-hour ago."

So he would know it was about the same time Dianne and he had been concluding their tryst.

She heard Graham take a quick impatient breath, then

say, "Look, Harrison, this is getting to be ridiculous. I'm interested in Amanda and I have to go pussyfooting around like an illicit lover. You clearly have your own amorous interests. Why not leave the field to me? If you were any sort of a sport, you'd depart the ship in Auckland. You certainly can't expect Amanda to go. How about it?"

"Not a chance, brother. I planned on making this trip, I'm going to make it—all the way. What you feel about Amanda is your business and maybe hers," Wynne added slowly. "But if you have any foolish dream of losing me, forget it. Sorry to seem uncooperative, but might as well be honest." He started to walk away, but turned long enough to say, "See you later, Amanda, I presume. Good night, Moore."

Graham stood watching him go. "What a guy!" he snorted. "How do you put up with him, Amanda? Is the trip really worth it?"

"Sometimes I wonder," she said slowly.

When Amanda returned to the stateroom later, Wynne had already retired. He was propped up in bed, light on, reading. "Would have come down to open the door, but I thought it was safer for me to just tell you to come on in with your key," he said sociably. "Didn't want to offend your sensibilities with my appearing in my pajamas."

She said nothing, but walked quietly across the room to her closet. Was it her imagination, or did she really catch the scent of perfume in the air, a lingering reminder of Dianne's presence?

When she padded out of the bathroom in her robe, to get into bed, Wynne said affably, "How'd you like what you saw of Auckland?"

"All right," she said shortly.

There was a pause. Then he leaned over the side of

his bed to say, "Still sore about my breaking up your little tête-à-tête a while ago?"

She made no comment.

"Look, Amanda, you didn't expect me to pack my gear and get out just on his suggestion, did you? You know why I'm here. You know why I'm going to stay until I finish my job. Meantime, let's just not get either of us kicked out of this room, or off the ship, by our actions concerning folks of the opposite sex, acting in a way that will make the purser feel pushed to take a moralistic stand."

"You should talk," she exploded.

His head suddenly reappeared over the edge of his bed, his eyes peering down at her. "Now, what is that supposed to mean?"

"How dumb do you think I am?" She forced herself to speak as calmly as she could. Which was not really very calm at all.

"Answering that is going to get me in trouble, my dear Amanda. But—out with it—what's bugging you?"

Keep quiet, she warned herself sternly. It didn't work. "Did you get your phone call, the one you stayed on board ship to get?"

"I did." He peered at her. "Come on, let's have it. Tell old Uncle Wynne what's got you up in the air."

Amanda felt like she was running around, trying to shore up a dam that kept threatening to break in a dozen different places. What good would it do to tell him why she felt as she did? At the same time she kept wanting to burst out in words. Here he was, acting as if he were a paragon of purity. As if nothing unusual was going on. Her lips tightened stubbornly. What really made her mad, she decided, was the way he had cleverly stage-managed the whole thing, getting her out of the way so he could devote himself to his little romance undisturbed.

Not for anything in the world would she allow him to know she had discovered his little amorous dalliance of this evening.

"Giving me the silent treatment, are you? Don't be a sorehead, Amanda Conklin," he said, drawing back his head, disappearing from her view, settling down again in his upper bunk.

She turned out her light and lay back on her pillow, not entirely certain if she were angry because of his lying to her, or because she now had to accept the end of any possible dream she had secretly held.

Suddenly he spoke again, "Going to make the all-day trip to the Glow-Worm Grotto tomorrow?"

"No," she replied distantly, "I don't plan to." It was one of the things she wanted to do, but could not afford.

"U'mm," he said, "I just wondered."

No doubt so he could entertain Dianne in this room again for an uninterrupted nine hours.

That, apparently, ended the conversation for the night. She heard only the turning of pages, then a little later the sound of his light turning off.

Morning found Wynne as cheery as if nothing had happened. At least, he seemed so on the surface. But under his banter she was still conscious there was that faintly withdrawn manner that had been in evidence ever since they had left Tahiti.

When they had finished breakfast, he tossed an envelope over to her. "Little present," he said.

They were dining alone, the others hadn't yet appeared. She took the envelope, giving him a puzzled look. Opening it, Amanda found a ticket for the Glow-Worm Grotto trip.

"This—is—is—for me?" she stammered. At his nod, she started shaking her head. "But I can't accept this. I—"

He held up his hand to stop her protests. "Peace offering."

His words brought a rise of bitterness to the back of her throat as her thoughts flew back to Dianne's secretive slipping away from her date with Wynne yesterday. Was this ticket to be certain that the two of them would have another undisturbed day?

"But I really can't take it. I know they cost quite a little bit and you shouldn't have done it. Maybe they will take it back," she said thinly.

He leaned across the table, blue eyes steady. "I know you are making the trip on a limited budget. This is a tour you really ought not to miss. So, okay, if I want to do this, why not let me? If you don't want to accept it as a peace offering, then let me call it my Boy Scout good deed of the day."

He was so pleasantly firm about it that she had difficulty in finding the gracious way to refuse. Then she handed it back across the table. "You use it, Wynne. Please, I'd feel better about it. I plan to spend the day in town looking around." That was just to signify she'd be out of the way, if it was all that important to get rid of her.

Wynne grinned and pulled a ticket out of his pocket. "I have one. They probably won't take it back. No use wasting it, is there? Amanda, don't be so stiff-necked and almighty proud."

The Babcocks arrived before Amanda could make any reply. "How's your eye, Tina?" Amanda inquired.

Tina smiled. "Perfectly all right now. It was some sort of cinder. The doctor had it out in seconds. You two going to the Glow-Worm Grotto?"

Wynne flashed a quick look at Amanda. "I guess so, aren't we, Amanda?"

"I—I think so," she said, capitulating because there seemed little else to do.

"Maybe we'll be on the same bus," the two Babcocks said as Wynne and Amanda rose to leave.

At the door of the salon they encountered Dianne on her way into breakfast. The red-haired girl's eyes went at once to Wynne. "Hello, Wynne, and you, too, Amanda," she added almost as an afterthought. "Going on the tour?"

"Sure. Are you?" offered Wynne politely, stepping aside to let the girl pass.

"Wouldn't miss it, after all you told me about it, Wynne," Dianne said.

Just as if I were not here at all, Amanda thought. She ignores me, almost deliberately.

There was nearly an hour to wait before the arrival of the tour buses. Amanda spent the time in writing post-cards to her friends back in Arizona. In a spirit of amia-bility, she even addressed one to her boss, Mr. Leland. She could almost hear his "Humph! Silly sentimentality and a waste of good money, that trip!"

As Amanda went down to the purser's office to mail the cards, she saw, to her surprise, Wynne deep in con-versation with Harry Shields. They were speaking in low serious tones, seemingly oblivious to others around them. She stuck the cards in the letter slot of the desk and turned away, a puzzled frown on her face. After the doubts both she and Wynne seemed to have about the man, it was strange to see the two together, clearly en-grossed in an intent discussion.

But Wynne hadn't noticed her and said nothing about Harry Shields when he knocked on the stateroom door later to tell her the tour was to start.

Several buses awaited as the passengers filed down the gangway. A shock-haired, red-cheeked guide, clad in gray wool knee-length sox and walking shorts, greeted Amanda and Wynne cheerfully as they boarded his bus. Amanda saw Graham enter, eyes raking the rows of seats to come to rest upon her for a second, then he took a seat toward the very front.

The motor started and the heavy vehicle lumbered through the congested city streets, then out into the suburbs, the drive punctuated by the guide's explanations of the local landmarks.

Great sweeps of green countryside began flashing past their windows, the hills dotted by tufts of what appeared to be moving white flowers but turned out to be sheep grazing along.

"It's so breathlessly beautiful!" Amanda turned impulsively toward Wynne, eyes shining.

He reached over to pat her hand, sending her pulse racing unevenly. "Glad you came, you stubborn little goose?" His smile robbed his comment of any possible sting.

She nodded happily, conscious that he had not taken his hand away. "It's so clean and open and so green, so very unbelievably green."

He was still smiling as he looked down at her, then slowly the smile faded away, blue eyes going abruptly deep and unreadable as he casually withdrew his hand. "Glad you're enjoying it," he said almost bluntly.

Something inside of her recoiled. Not that she had been either deceived or encouraged by the touch of his hand for that extra moment, she assured herself, but his withdrawal was both physical and mental. Again he had that odd look that she had become accustomed to seeing of late. And if he were erecting a firm invisible barrier between them, almost a subtle warning she was not to trespass.

As they drove along, her forehead often pressed to the windowpane lest she miss some of the countryside, her mind became truant, flitting back intermittently to that surprising meeting between Wynne and Harry Shields. In the very back of her thoughts, a small dark shadow began to spread. Surely Wynne and that dreadful man could have nothing in common except—except— Her

eyes lifted and she could catch the reflection of Wynne's
face in the glass. For a moment she would not allow the
sickening thought to push forward. Amanda bit tensely
at her lower lip. Wynne had said there were two of the
diamond thieves who hadn't been caught. She had
thought Harry Shields might be one of them. Wynne's
profile moved in the reflecting glass window. Was
Wynne the other one? There, she thought bitterly, she
had opened the Pandora's box! Maybe he had misled her
all along and this search of his for a secret object was
not for an insurance company, but for himself alone.

She twisted her hands together tensely in her lap,
doubt reaching out long tentacles like an octopus. She
felt like a miserable traitor, to be sitting here, accepting
the favor of this special and not inexpensive trip, and
thinking the things that she was.

Then, slowly, her volatile emotional state began to
steady itself. Wynne was not a thief. Whatever else he
was, however much he had evaded the truth about Dianne, he was not a criminal, she was convinced of that.

But other things troubled her. Since Tahiti his attitude
toward her was different. And there was also the way he
had managed to get her out of the way last night on the
hollow pretext of a phone call—then having Dianne in
his room. There was something so deceitful and disillusioning in the manner he had gone about that.

Amanda leaned back in her seat, eyes fixed unseeingly
on the passing scenery. Way in the deepest part of her
mind, she recognized now, reluctantly but surely, what
she must do. In spite of everything, her long-awaited
dream, she was not going on with the trip.

She felt a wave of utter sickness and despair wash
over her. Perhaps the situation had never been right
from the very first. And for days now she had tried to
fool herself, to refuse to see how unwise, how ill-fated,
and how absolutely hopeless it all was.

How could she bear to go on, staying in the same room, night after night, with the man to whom she had lost her heart, and feel she had to keep up a constant shield across her emotions lest she inadvertently reveal to him how she felt? It was not becoming easier, it was becoming more difficult.

And so she was going home. From Auckland. The very thought gave her an all-gone sensation at the pit of her stomach. She ran over in her mind every single penny she could possibly scrape up. All the meager amount she had so carefully calculated for the small necessities and the short trips ashore. Enough? For the very cheapest of tourists' flights home? She wasn't sure. Probably it was not. Still, there was one thing she could do as a last resort. She could wire Mr. Carr at the bank back home. He knew her, he had been a friend of her father's. It wouldn't be for much, she would hate to ask, but he would send it, she knew.

"Penny for your thoughts, or in these days of inflation, shall we say a dime?" Wynne's voice startled her.

If he only knew what she was thinking! "No thoughts," she replied in a small flat voice.

"Pretty grim face for no thoughts," he said curiously.

Was she a fool to take such a rash step? To leave? No. It was the only thing to do now. The whole cruise had lost its appeal, almost its meaning. Why should she go on now with this self-torture, loving him and trying to conceal it from him? It had simply become impossible to continue.

She made up her mind to say nothing about it now. She would not tell Wynne until tonight, after they returned to the ship and she was ready to pack. Maybe— maybe, she thought morosely, she'd better just leave a note.

The bus pulled up in front of a small gabled teahouse and everyone piled out to enter and seat themselves at

tables. Amanda managed to smile and chat with everyone around her, but she had the feeling she was two
people: one on the surface, sociable and affable; the
other one, inside, was in pure misery. She was conscious
that from time to time Wynne gazed at her with a questioning look in his eyes. She didn't care, not anymore,
she thought unhappily and not very truthfully. She *did*
care, and that was what hurt.

Afterward, before the bus loaded again, they all
strolled around the gardens. Graham came up beside her
while Wynne was purchasing some postcards at a store
nearby.

"This is what I mean, Amanda. Here I am, trailing
along like a frustrated bill collector, while Wynne, who
really has no special right, gets to squire you about at
will. Right now, let's plan on getting together tonight
when we get back. We'll slip out and have a quiet dinner somewhere onshore."

"I—I—" she began, then hesitated. She ought to tell
Graham she was leaving; it wouldn't be so difficult to
say it to him, and he had been attentive to her. She gave
a quick look over her shoulder and could see Wynne
thumbing through cards on racks in the store window. "I
am afraid not, Graham. I'm going home."

"Home?" His eyebrows shot up. "Some emergency?"

"No, it's just that I've changed my mind. It hasn't
turned out quite like I planned."

"Harrison have anything to do with it?" Graham gestured with his head toward the store.

"It's a number of things, really. I just feel that I'd
rather go," she evaded.

Graham looked down at her, scrutinizing her face as if
searching out the real reason. She grew uncomfortable
under the intensity of his gaze.

"Does he know? Is he going with you?" The words
came out sharply.

"Oh, no, I don't want him to know." Amanda looked at him anxiously. "Please, don't say anything about it to anyone. I'll just leave."

Some of the passengers walked behind them, heading for the bus, once more to board. Wynne could be seen digging into his pockets to pay for his cards.

"When? Where? Leaving, I mean?" Graham's voice was tight, urgent, gray eyes darkening.

"As soon as we get back, today. I'll pack and go."

"But, it's so sudden, Amanda! And you're not telling him? Not at all?"

"I'm going to leave a note."

He tried again, hurriedly now, for Wynne was coming out of the store, walking toward them. "Why are you leaving really?"

It was too late for an answer, for Wynne called to her, "Let's go, Amanda, the bus is about to take off."

"I've got to go," she said hastily to Graham. "Thanks for everything. For this, too." Her hand touched the small heart he had given her. Then she had to leave, to join Wynne, who stood patiently waiting by the bus door. As she boarded, she regretted that her leavetaking from Graham had been so abrupt, but in a way it was better so. Otherwise, he might have tried to talk her out of it, or if that hadn't succeeded, he might wish to get in touch again after the trip. But that she didn't want. The trip would be over, unhappily, disillusioning; she would not want any further ties to remind her. Graham had been nice to her, had even been ardent in his pursuit, but—she frowned as she slid into her seat by the window—she had never really been entirely comfortable with him, even if she couldn't explain why to herself.

"Everybody here?" The tour guide stood in the front, looking down the aisles, counting heads. Then, apparently assured, he motioned to the driver, who started the motor, and the bus rumbled down the road, the

guide picking up his microphone and informing them
when they would be reaching the Glow-Worm Grotto
and the other places they would be seeing along the
way.

"What was the problem?" Wynne broke into Amanda's
thoughts.

She turned to face him. "What problem?" she asked
flatly, disconcerted by his abrupt tone.

He nodded toward the front of the bus. "Your
boyfriend, Graham. Sure, don't tell me, I know it's none
of my business; we've done that one several times, but it
looked to me like Moore had something on his mind that
was causing him to glower. Plenty. I'm not trying to butt
into your private life, but if he's giving trouble... ?"

"Graham? No, *he* isn't!" Then she shut her mouth
abruptly. That was the wrong thing to say, the wrong
way to accent it.

And he got it. Answering the meaning that came
through her words, he said dryly, "I see." He settled
back in the seat, his eyes focused on the window,
watching the verdant countryside slide past, his expression a picture of controlled coolness and disinterest.

At the next bus stop, for luncheon, Wynne was rigidly
and distantly polite. Smoldering, she thought suddenly.
Her words had come out like a brisk rebuff, she realized
that, but she hadn't meant it quite the way he had taken
it. As she stepped from the bus onto the pavement leading to the restaurant, she felt regret, she should say
something to Wynne, apologize, say he hadn't gotten her
true meaning, but she couldn't, for then she would have
to say what her inner meaning was. And that would
never do.

After the luncheon, eaten under restrained conversation, overpolite to each other, they climbed into the bus
for the final lap to the grotto.

Wynne turned to her as they seated themselves. "I

hadn't realized how distasteful my company has become to you. Perhaps I'm not sensitive enough to get the real lack of vibes between us. I'll try not to inflict myself on you more than necessary from now on," he said stiffly.

"It's not—" she started, then stopped, what was the use saying more? It didn't matter now. She certainly couldn't explain that she had fallen in love with him and that that was the real source of her problem.

So Amanda sat silent, feeling completely miserable, more than ever convinced she had made the right decision about leaving. Yet it left little room for happiness. Her eyes stung hotly, terrifying her that she might actually cry. But she squinted her eyes tightly once or twice, passed a surreptitious hand swiftly across them, and managed to do away with any signs of emotion.

There were two other tour buses pulled up in the large parking area at the Glow-Worm Grotto. The guide rose to his feet and faced the passengers in their bus. "Please try to stay together, ladies and gentlemen. The Waitomo Caves, where we will find the Glow-Worm Grotto, are filled with winding passageways, honeycombing a large area. I brought you all here, I'd be happy to be able to take you all back with me." He grinned at them. "Don't be adventuresome."

He was quite right about the winding passageways, Amanda realized as they entered the damp cool air of the grayish-white cave. The tour guide handed his passengers over to the cave guide, who repeated the warning about staying together. "One wrong turn, if you stray off by yourself, and quick as 'Bob's your uncle' you'll be lost. Now, come on, everyone, follow me." With that, he started off, down a long tunnel, eerie-looking in the dim lights, stalactites reaching like ghostly gray fingers down at the tourists passing underneath. In places, stalagmites thrust their points up from the ground as if struggling to reach up to the stalactites and block the entrance of some of the tunnels to the intruding tourists. There was something so weird and otherworldly about the endless pathways that Amanda noticed an unnatural silence falling over the group; often the only sound was the shuffle of their shoes over the limestone trail, the slow drip-drip of moisture falling from the stalactites. Amanda felt a ripple of a cool shiver run between her shoulders, not entirely due to the cave's faint chill.

Wynne made no effort to remain by her side as he had before, clearly following his comment about not inflicting himself on her. Ahead, too, were the Babcocks, who had come on an earlier bus. The path led up inclines, twisting around grotesque limestone formations, endless caverns opening up in the distance.

Now they were approaching a large chamber with a long flight of steps leading down to a darkened entrance to still another tunnel. As they entered that one, dim lights gave a ghostly glow to the path.

The guide stopped. His voice was low. "Now we must ask for absolute silence. No lights of any kind, please, flash cameras or cigarette lighters, as we approach the underground river to the Glow-Worm Grotto. Follow me."

Obediently the tourists straggled along in single file as they descended to a small wooden dock that was barely visible in the shadowy area. One by one they were helped into the flat-bottom boats, Amanda carefully feeling her way, along with the rest, crowding side by side onto the damp wooden seats. Then even the dim glow vanished as the few lights were extinguished, plunging everything into profound darkness. Softly cautioning them once more to absolute silence, the boatman began moving the boat away from the jetty, using overhead wires to pull it along, hand over hand, the only sound the quiet movement through the lapping water. Amanda found herself holding her breath in anticipation as the slow-moving craft made a turn at the bend in the river to suddenly enter a large cavern.

Her eyes caught the first glimpse of the magic above her, the glowing blue-green radiance given off by tens of thousands of insect larvae clinging to the roof and walls, turning the stalactites into sparkling chandeliers, the endless brilliance reflecting in the smooth dark waters below.

Silently the boat moved along the river as heads craned upward, staring at the star-studded ceiling. If she saw no more, Amanda thought, this would have made the whole trip worthwhile. It was as if she had been temporarily transported into a fantastically beautiful dreamworld, the real world far removed from her and her troubled mind.

There was not a sound but the quiet lap of the water as the boat was pulled through it by the man hauling on the wire. The cavern was vast, but at last the craft began circling around to return, the passengers twisting their heads to take a last look at the enchantment they were leaving behind them.

When they got back to the jetty, Amanda fumbled her way out of the boat and up onto the wooden platform. In the dim light Wynne was not visible. Several flat-bottom craft carried spectators, so he could easily have been in one of the others still making their way into the sparkling cavern. Was he with Dianne, she wondered fleetingly, then put the thought out of her mind. It didn't matter now. She waited about for a moment, then shrugged and went on up the stairs, tagging along at the end of the single-file group, passing through a large limestone chamber, then on into a winding tunnel.

"Amanda." It was scarcely a whisper.

She halted, looking around quickly. The sound had come from in back of her, but there was no one there. Then it came again. "Amanda."

She cocked her head, listening, puzzled. The call, soft but urgent, seemed to be coming somewhere to the right, a short distance behind her. But all she could see was one of the numerous bypaths, looking much like others she had seen, twisting and grotesque in the muted light.

The group she had been following had moved some distance ahead. She hesitated, uncertain, then twisted her head to gaze once more in the direction from which the voice had come.

"Amanda, help me, please!" Now there was panic in the fading sound, so weak a plea she could barely make it out. The last word was only partly formed. Then silence, broken only by the drip of water on limestone.

She reminded herself that she couldn't lose her way if she kept the main path within sight; so, acting on worried impulse, she bolted quickly back and into the curving pathway, the ghostly stalactites, like giant fungi, hanging from the dark arch of the roof.

There was no sound now. Amanda halted as she rounded a small curve of the trail. "Yes?" she called in a thin shaking voice. "Who is it? Where are you?"

There was no reply—and no warning.

Amanda did not feel the blow. It was more like an explosion inside her head, great streaking shards of lights flashed, then there was nothing but black endless night.

Chapter 10

Small prickles of light began creeping under Amanda's eyelids. Her lashes fluttered, opened to glaring brightness, then closed again. Thoughts floated helplessly within her mind as she struggled back to consciousness.

"Amanda." Wynne's voice came cutting through her mental fog. Her lashes lifted once again, eyes blinking defensively against the harsh circle of light.

"Amanda. Are you all right?" It was Wynne again, his voice anxious. She felt her head and shoulders being elevated to brace against the warmth of his chest and arms.

Slowly, dizzily, she raised her eyes. Wynne's face floated cloudily above her, an aureole of brightness in back of his head.

"Yes, yes, I think so," her voice was a whisper.

"My God, you little fool! Where did you think you were going? Didn't you hear the guide when he warned everyone not to stray off the main path?" His gruff scolding did not hide his anxiety.

"I didn't stray; someone called me," she protested weakly.

Abruptly she was aware that there were others about, a circle of people around them, men with lanterns and flashlights. She struggled to sit up, but the sudden movement sent pain down her neck and shoulders and along her cheekbones. A giant vise seemed to tighten around her head.

"Stay still until we can get you out of here," Wynne said rebukingly, his arms cradling her more firmly. She could hear the steady hard beat of his heart. His nearness made her own heart quicken, pulsing uncomfortably through her already aching head.

"Called? You say someone called? There's no one here," he said.

She tried to remember. "I—someone—I thought someone was in trouble. They called. Are you sure there isn't anyone back there?" she managed worriedly.

Several of the men detached themselves from the group to go flashing their lights down the path, their footsteps echoing until they could be heard no longer.

"Do you feel like being moved now?" Wynne asked, shifting her slightly in his arms as if trying to make her more comfortable.

"I—I think so. In a minute I can try." She stirred.

"Not get up! I don't mean that! We'll carry you out. You got one hell of a bump when you ran into that stalactite up there." He looked up.

The icicle-shaped object dangling above them had the point broken and it lay a few feet from her, she discovered, as she slowly moved her eyes about.

Then something caught at her consciousness. What was it? She tried to think as she gazed up at the limestone cone. But Wynne and one of the other men were talking and she couldn't seem to concentrate.

Now there was the sound of more footsteps and two men arrived with a stretcher that they put down on the floor beside her. At almost the same moment, the men who had pushed farther down the byway in search of the person who had called to her came back, lanterns and flashlights sending weird shadows swinging up the vaulted walls.

"Nothing. No one. Comes to a full stop back there," they reported.

Amanda was being gently lifted onto the stretcher, though she continued to feebly protest that she thought she could walk. All at once she began feeling feverishly about her. "My purse," she said worriedly.

"I'll find it," Wynne assured her and moved back from the stretcher. She heard some of the other men stir, too, flashing the lights about.

"I found it." How strange Wynne's voice sounded, she thought fleetingly. After a moment's hesitation, he was back at her side. "I'll hold on to your purse for you," he told her as the men carrying the stretcher began moving, slowly trudging back along the path, stopping shortly to back and fill, edging her around a sharp angle, going a short distance, then repeating the same painstaking action as they came to another angle.

Abruptly realization burst in her mind. "Wynne!" She beckoned tremulously for him to come nearer. "Wynne, we haven't reached the main path yet? We're still on the side one?"

"Yes," she said briefly. Why did he sound so odd, almost angry, she wondered?

But she continued, "I didn't walk this far, just a little distance, around one corner. I remember. I wasn't where you found me when—" She halted, wrinkling her forehead, trying to think. The movement pained, so she relaxed the tightened muscles but she couldn't wipe away the puzzling question in her mind. When she—what?

Bit by bit she picked at the tag ends hanging from the knot in the back of her consciousness. She had walked just a short distance, only feet from the main path, rounded a corner, and—and— She was frustrated, nothing at all was clear from then on.

The stretcher moved into the main lighted chamber. It

had taken this much time to get here, she thought, so
she was right: where she was found was some distance!
Perhaps she could have stumbled into the stalactite
without seeing it, perhaps, but how had she gotten so
far beyond the place she remembered so clearly?

Wynne was talking to the men and discussing the possibility of using an ambulance.

"No," she said. "I don't need, I don't want, an ambulance. My head aches. That's all. I don't want an ambulance. I'll go back in the bus with the rest."

"The bus has gone," Wynne replied tersely. "If you
won't agree to an ambulance and going to a hospital, I'll
rent a car to take you back."

Automatically she started to protest, but realized that
it was the lesser of two evils to go back in a rented car.
She certainly didn't need an ambulance. Any more than
Wynne needed an ambulance when the coconut fell on
his head in Moorea.

A sudden stunning thought mushroomed in Amanda's
mind. Wynne said he hadn't been under the tree when
the coconut fell. Then, perhaps, she hadn't been hurt by
bumping into a stalactite. It had broken off, but that
didn't mean anything. The cone tip had been found near
her, as the coconut had been lying by Wynne. He'd
guessed it had been thrown at him in an attempt to
maim, perhaps to kill, at the very least to warn him off.
But why would anyone want to hurt her? And, if someone did, it had to be a person she knew, someone who
had known her name.

But her thoughts were interrupted by the arrival of a
doctor who had been summoned by one of the cave offi-
cials. The thin, angular-jawed man, with gray hair and
surprisingly gentle eyes, examined her injury in one of
the small buildings at the foot of the trail.

In the light of the room, she glanced down to see her

blouse was unbuttoned. With hurried fingers she started to fasten it while the doctor was examining her injury.

"Some laceration of the scalp, young lady, a nasty raised place. We're going to have to clean the area and use an antiseptic lotion." He got out some bottles and Amanda gritted her teeth to the stinging of the liquid.

"Now, I think that should do for the moment. Best you don't exert yourself for a few days, however." He paused. "Unless you'd rather go into the hospital for a complete thorough examination?"

"No," she rushed to assure him, "I'll be quite all right. If you think it's needed, I can see the ship's doctor."

He nodded. "Right. Now let's wait a few moments to see if the bleeding has indeed stopped. It didn't bleed a lot, but we want to be certain it won't."

The moments dragged slowly by. Amanda wanted to be off, but she kept her eye on the doctor, waiting for him to say she could go. Finally he seemed satisfied and nodded at her. "Very well, but do be careful about trying to do too much for another few days." He smiled at her. "And don't forget to see your ship's physician."

Wynne was waiting outside with the rented car. "Do you feel like starting now?" he asked.

"Yes," she said sturdily, as two men who worked at the cave helped her into the car.

She thanked them and brushed off all concern about her injury, assuring them no one was to blame but herself for having strayed off the main path. She thanked those who had searched for her, her lips forming the words politely, but her mind was spinning like a whirlwind. All she wanted now was to get away from here, to talk to Wynne alone, bringing up the shattering possibility she was struggling with in her thoughts.

"You sure you feel all right?" Wynne asked worriedly as he backed the car around and prepared to head for Auckland and the ship.

"Of course. Sorry to take so long, but the doctor wanted me to wait." Then she could hold back no longer. "Wynne, something—something I'm not sure of—but I don't think it was an accident! I'm almost positive I didn't run into that stalactite. And I know I hadn't gone that far along the pathway to the point where you found me."

Amanda saw his hands tighten on the steering wheel, his eyes fixed on the road ahead. For a moment he didn't answer. Then he said simply, "I think you're right. Let me show you something. I've got your purse here beside me. Here, take a look at it before we discuss anything else."

He fumbled by his side, then picked up the purse to hand it to her, his eyes not swerving from the highway in front of them.

She took it, puzzled by the note of strain in his voice.

"Look in it, Amanda."

She undid the clasp, her eyes widening as she saw the lining was ripped loose, the small mirror in her compact shattered and partly removed, everything that had been in her brown wallet had been dumped into the bottom of her purse.

"I tried to scoop up everything from the floor of the cave. Pretty sure I got it all. Sorry I didn't have time to do more than stuff it into your purse."

"Wynne!" Realization ran a cold chill through her. "Someone thought I had it, didn't they? The thing from our stateroom?"

He nodded. "That's what it looks like. Of course we can't rule out a simple attempt at mugging. Robbery." His voice didn't sound as if he believed that.

But Amanda searched her purse again, then said slowly, "No, my money is all here. And whoever it was called me, called me by name."

"They tried to set up a scene of an accident for me on

Moorea," Wynne said. "Now they try the same type of thing on you. That's the way criminals tend to act, repeating the same method. *Modus operandi*, the police term it."

He turned his head briefly to look at her. "Amanda, this is no place for you now. I mean, the cruise. Why not leave in Auckland? This is a criminal operation, and it wouldn't be the first time an innocent person got hurt—one way or another. I'd hate to see it happen to you." He bit off the words sharply.

But she had already planned on leaving in Auckland! The decision to do so had momentarily been startled from her mind by what had happened. Amanda stared ahead, her eyes seeing the rich green countryside, but her mind wasn't registering it. If anything, this attack on her should only further encourage her desire to go. Why, then, did she suddenly feel a new reluctance?

"How did you find me?" she asked, wanting now to steer the conversation away from the matter of her leaving, her emotions still too uncertain for her to trust them not to betray her real reason for going.

"When I got back on the bus and found you weren't there, I waited until everyone had boarded and the guide asked if anyone knew where you were. I kept thinking you'd be rushing up at the last minute, that you'd gotten behind or had stopped to buy postcards at the stand near the gate. I got out of my seat to go forward to ask your friend Graham, but he said he hadn't seen you either."

Wynne slowed the car as they entered a small town, putting on the brakes and stopping from time to time as schoolchildren scampered across the road.

After they were out on the open highway again, he went back to his conversation. "I had a weird feeling, Amanda, of something wrong. I'm not speaking only about your not arriving at the bus, but—well, call it a sense of uneasiness. I got out of the bus and told the tour guide not to delay all the other passengers, to go ahead, that I'd find you and we'd return by car. He was reluctant, but he had a schedule he was trying to stick to, and he'd already done a fair amount of waiting for you, so he finally agreed."

"So you came back to the cave? How did you know where to find me?"

"God! Find you?" he exploded. "It was luck, pure un-adulterated luck. Why, unless you had regained consciousness and struggled out on your own, you could have lain where you were until kingdom come! And, if you had been hurt worse, you might have. We might have still been searching; there are hundreds of off-trails. But, before I left the bus, I asked when you had been seen last by anyone, and your elderly friend, Mrs. Stewart, said you had been in her boat and had started up the stairs with the rest of the group. So the guides and I began our search from there on."

"Wynne"—nerves made Amanda's voice tremble—"who was it?"

There was a long silence. She looked at his stern profile. "Do you know?" she asked, this time a bit more steadily, more insistently. Somehow she had the feeling that he did.

"It's not something you can go around making a wild guess about, Amanda. Let's say I'm fairly certain. But fairly certain isn't enough to actually indict someone, so let's leave it at that for the moment."

She saw his jaw muscles tighten. "But let's get back to you and the matter of leaving the trip in Auckland," he said firmly. "I know how you feel about the cruise, but now there are some pretty valid reasons for you to reconsider your decision. There's your safety, for one thing, and there's another possibility—" He hesitated on the brink of saying something, then gave an odd shake of the head, not finishing the sentence.

"What were you going to say?" she questioned.

"Nothing," he said bluntly. "It's just that I think you should take my advice."

She made no reply, partly because she didn't know what to say. Should I go, she wondered? Probably. But not for the reasons he had said—or hadn't said. What was wrong with her? She'd planned on going, why was she wasting further thought on it? Besides, it was hard to think right now, her mind and her will seemed suddenly flaccid. Leaning back against the seat, she closed her eyes against the glare of the sunset.

"You feel all right?" Wynne voiced concern. "Maybe we shouldn't have tried—"

"I'm all right, yes. I've a headache, but it isn't so bad now." That was meant to reassure Wynne. It did hurt, but it wasn't unbearable. The only trouble was that she seemed to have lost the ability to think through the frightening questions that crowded the edge of her mind. She wanted to rest, but she could not. Who had called to her? Had it been a man's voice or a woman's? She tried to make herself recall that soft anguished cry, but the pounding at her temples got in the way.

Her uneasy confused thoughts kept returning again and again to gnaw nervously at the questions. Abruptly her eyes widened.

"Wynne, it almost had to be a man. A woman wouldn't have found it easy to drag me any distance after knocking me out."

"Right, I'd say so. A woman could have, but I suspect it was a man."

"Harry Shields, he could have. He's strong enough, he's—" she began, but Wynne cut her words off decisively.

"He wasn't on the tour. Stayed on the ship."

There was *that* question again, too. Why had he and Wynne been talking so seriously? She closed her eyes. Every question that came up dragged a dozen more in its wake, and her mind simply didn't seem to be able to grapple with any of them, she thought querulously.

Once or twice she opened her eyes to look appraisingly at Wynne. His face was so closed, so devoid of expression. And, she reflected bitterly, so dear. Why had she fallen in love with him? He was brusque, varying only by being blightingly casual toward her. His nearness sped her heart, but brought her little comfort.

Wynne took the shortest way back to the ship, slicing miles off the more picturesque route, driving with intent preoccupation that she found difficult to penetrate.

Once or twice she made futile attempts to question him on some of the things that hung unanswered in her mind, things she felt he knew, but he only turned them aside, saying, "Amanda, you ought to rest, not worry about those subjects right now. We can talk everything over later." With that, he would concentrate more intently on his driving, his lips straightening into a firm stubborn line.

At last they reached the outskirts of Auckland, to be instantly enmeshed in heavy evening traffic, their car caught in a series of stop-and-go lights until they finally came to the docks and, turning in through the gates, reached their ship.

Wynne hopped out of the car and came around to assist Amanda to her feet. For a second she swayed, the trip after the accident leaving her a little tired and dizzy. But the moment passed, the horizon stopped revolving about her, and she gave Wynne a wobbly smile.

"Sorry about that," she said, "I'm not used to being hit on the head. I can't say much for it."

His hand on her arm tightened. She hoped he couldn't

hear the ridiculous pounding of her heart at his touch, it was certainly loud enough in her own ears.

"Now, right to the doctor's office for you," he ordered as they went slowly up the gangway.

"Wynne, but—I—" she attempted, but was overruled by the simple action of his steering her firmly through the foyer and down the short hall to the doctor.

Wynne gave the medical man a rather abridged report on the incident, carefully avoiding any reference to possible foul play. Then he turned to Amanda. "I'll come back for you when the doctor has finished. Wait here for me!" It was clearly an order.

"But—" she started to protest. If she wanted to leave the ship here in Auckland, she had things to do and not a lot of time to do them.

"No, Amanda, wait. I'll feel better about it if you do. She really shouldn't go wandering off to the room unescorted, Doctor," Wynne sounded every bit the concerned husband. "She might get dizzy and faint, she was a little light-headed when we got out of the car. I'll be back for her shortly,"

The doctor gave Wynne an approving smile. He clearly approved of such marital consideration. "Don't worry, young man, she'll be here, I'll see to it."

There was little Amanda could do, the matter clearly had been taken out of her hands. She felt faintly sulky. Had Wynne been concerned for her purely because of affection, that was one thing, but she had a feeling that he didn't want her underfoot in the stateroom . . . or elsewhere for a while. Was he treating her like a bothersome child or a handicap to a romantic tryst with Dianne? Either way, it was irritating. So she almost grudgingly submitted to an exhaustive examination by the doctor. He heard the office door close behind Wynne as he left.

"Wicked bump on your head there." The doctor's fingers gently moved on her scalp. "No bleeding now, though. But I bet you had, maybe still have, a king-sized headache. Weird kind of accident, come to think of it. Don't think I've ever encountered a stalactite one before." He peered down at her head. "Strange you didn't get a laceration or some kind of bruise on your forehead when you ran into it." He straightened, rubbing his jaw thoughtfully with his hand. "You know, I think it fell on you, rather than your running into it, or do you recall hitting it?" He gazed at her questioningly.

"I—I don't remember," she managed truthfully enough, her mind leaping to the confirmation of her suspicions. Of course she had been hit by someone, she had never really thought otherwise. "All I can recall was having something burst out like bright lights in my head, and that's all I knew," Amanda told the doctor.

After completing the examination, he gave her much the same advice as the doctor back at the caves: to rest, to take it easy for a while. Then he added he would like to see her again tomorrow, just to confirm his opinion that everything was all right, and no complications because of her injury. He gave her a sympathetic smile. "If you can call having a bump like that 'all right,'" he told her. "I imagine it doesn't feel very comfortable."

She assured him it wasn't too bad, and looked hopefully toward the door.

He shook a playful finger at her. "No, I'm responsible for you. I promised your husband you would be here."

So she sat in the waiting room, restless to be out and away at her packing. It was only then that she realized she had reaffirmed her decision to leave. If not tonight, then tomorrow, after seeing the doctor again as he requested, but before the ship sailed in the afternoon. Doing it that way, she realized, meant spending one more night in the same room with Wynne, a difficult night, knowing she would not be seing him ever again.

And it would be hard, she knew that. How carefully

must she discipline her unhappy heart and not let the thought of farewell betray her to a man who had so clearly stated she was not his type, and followed up his statement by a clear demonstration. Amanda gazed down at her rumpled skirt, then lifted her eyes to look out toward the foyer, waiting. Dianne, she reflected, would have the field to herself now.

It seemed that she had been in the doctor's office a very long time. Amanda glanced at her wristwatch, then out the door again, hoping that Wynne would be coming into sight at any moment. The situation wasn't improved by the doctor sticking his head out the office door and viewing her with some surprise.

"Still here, young lady? Well, don't worry, he'll be back shortly, I'm certain. Meantime, why not look at a magazine to pass the time?"

She thanked him, reached over to a nearby table, picking up a magazine at random, not even bothering to see what it was, and opened it up on her lap; the doctor nodded approvingly as he withdrew his head. But she made no effort to read or even look at the pages. Where was Wynne?

From the foyer, where passengers were arriving or leaving the ship for the evening, there began a most peculiar sound. Amanda strained to see and hear. A murmur rose and grew like a garbled wave of voices. From where she was sitting, Amanda could see only a corner of the foyer, but the people in her line of vision seemed to be pulling back from the center of the room. Amanda rose to go to the door, to stand looking out.

The focus of everyone's attention seemed to be on something or someone at the far end of the room. Amanda could not see what it was. She hesitated, then impulsively decided to find out, regardless of Wynne's instructions to remain where she was.

Before she had taken more than a step outside the

door, she saw Wynne and Harry Shields, their heads bent in deep conversation, oblivious to the people standing about. Wynne lifted his head suddenly, saw her, then held up a quick hand as if to halt her coming toward him. He spoke a word to Shields, then came hurrying across the foyer and down the short hall to where she stood.

"Amanda." His voice was sharp. "Go back inside, now! Wait there."

"But, Wynne—" she protested, disturbed at the hard lines about his mouth, the urgency of his manner.

"I'll explain later. Do as I say, Amanda," he ordered curtly.

It was too late. She saw.

Graham was coming through the foyer. But not alone. He was being escorted by a group of men, one of them in a policeman's uniform. Graham's face was pallid, as his head lifted, his eyes brushed hers for an infinitesimal second, then quickly turned away, leaving only a shadowy impression of . . . something. She could barely register it: was it apology . . . regret? She could not be sure, for she was too stunned to think.

Before she could utter a sound, there was a new wave of murmurs. And another group of serious-faced men crossing the foyer. This time, in their midst, Dianne, head imperious, manner arrogant. Graham's face had been gray and drawn, but hers was disdainful as her eyes swept coolly over the watching crowd.

"I tried to avoid having you witness this." Wynne took Amanda's arm. "I wanted to prepare you. Well"—he shrugged—"I was too late. Come on, we'll go back to the stateroom now and I'll try to fill you in on everything. Everything, that is, that I know so far."

Amanda was still dazed. "But, Graham, what has he done? And Dianne? They're being arrested, aren't they? Wynne . . . ?"

His voice was brusque but not unkind as he muttered, "Later, Amanda, let's get out of here first." With his hand at her elbow, he steered her down the hall in the opposite direction from the foyer, away from the spectators who still stood about, their voices shrill now with excitement and questions.

"We'll go around the other way," he said briskly.

Clearly he was going to say no more at the moment, so Amanda asked nothing further, waiting until they could reach the stateroom. As they paused outside the door, Wynne getting out his key, Amanda gave an unsteady glance toward the room across the hall. Graham. What had he done? She had a sickening premonition that she tried to shove away. Not Graham. Not at the cave. For an instant she shut her eyes as if thereby she could shut her mind.

Wynne stood back to allow her to enter. "Sorry about the room," he said.

Amanda stopped abruptly to stare. The room was a shambles, dresser drawers yawned open, their contents tossed on the dressing table, on the sofa, the floor. Closets, books, everything in disarray. Wynne closed the door behind them and began scooping garments off the sofa so that she could sit down.

He turned, facing her, stockings and sweaters in his hands. "Shall I go ahead and try to get things a bit in order or shall we talk first?"

"Talk!" She gazed up at him tensely. "Just drop those things of mine, I'll tend to them later. Wynne, I've got to know what's been going on."

He stood for a moment holding the handful of garments, looking about for some uncluttered place to set them, then he gave up and piled them on the rest of the scattered articles on the dressing table.

Hooking the chair with his foot, he dragged it over and sank into it. There was a pause before he said quietly, "I'm sorry, Amanda. Especially if you cared for him. It's tough to have you find out this way."

"But what did he do, you haven't said, is he ...? He's not one of the ...?" She didn't have to finish, she didn't even have to wait for his answer. She knew now.

"Yes. One of the original holdup men who robbed the jewelry store."

She found it hard to reconcile it in her mind. Not a holdup man, not a criminal—Graham? Amanda found it difficult to believe. Then, if it were true, today at the caves it had to be Graham who had attacked her, much as she had tried to turn her mind from the thought a moment ago.

"Harry Shields? Isn't he one of them, too? He was searching our room, too, wasn't he?" she asked.

Wynne gave her a twisted grin that held little humor. "Yep, he said he had a little look around, just checking. You know what Shields is? A cop! He's been on the case from the beginning. He's had his eye on Moore, had a tip-off on him as a possibility, so he used a little police influence to get assigned to the same room as the man he suspected. What better cover than to look like a— well, whatever he looked like—not a cop, anyhow? And he could have a twenty-four-hour watch on his suspect without having to find an excuse for it. To catch Moore rifling this room was all he needed."

Wynne leaned forward, clasping his hands in front of him, balancing them on his knees. "But Moore— Sorry to have it end like that for you, Amanda."

"Or you," she said quietly.

"What do you mean ... me?" He leaned back, eyebrows arching.

"Dianne. Was she, is she, Graham's wife or something? They took her too, didn't they?"

"Sure they took her. When they hauled Moore in, they picked her up, too. Don't you get it? She was the fourth thief. In these days it isn't too surprising, is it? After all, women have been going to jail for some pretty big crimes, haven't they?"

Was he covering his feelings by talking this way, Amanda wondered. "Don't you mind, Wynne? I mean . . ." she began cautiously.

His head drew back, cocking to one side questioningly. "I? But— Oh, for the love of Mike. You mean you think I had a serious thing going with Dianne, don't you?" He gave her a sheepish look. "Maybe that's what you were supposed to think. How could I tell you that I had had a tip-off about the chance there was a woman involved in the theft? There were some things I couldn't tell you in case you might inadvertently give it away. Sorry about that, but it had to be."

Amanda looked bewildered, so much was happening all at once.

"Another thing," Wynne said, "when you were so adamant about staying in this room, no matter what, I wondered if the girl in the case might not be you. But inquiries back in Arizona proved you were exactly what you said you were. We checked. And, too, Dianne came on so strong that I figured there had to be a reason for all that enthusiasm in my direction, that maybe it wasn't just for my handsome face and form, but for a chance to get into this room."

"But she . . . but you . . . ?" Amanda burst out impulsively, then stopped short.

"She and I what?" His blue eyes were suddenly alert.

"I—uh—" she began, then halted in confusion. She didn't want to go on, lest she somehow, inadvertently, give away the reason she hadn't said anything before. Maybe he still wasn't exactly frank about his relationship with Dianne.

"Out with it, Amanda. Dianne and I what?"

Reluctantly she told him. "Last night, when I came

back early from Auckland, I started for the room, but before I got to the door, I saw Dianne come around the corner from here, and I thought . . ."

"Last night? So she did get in to have a little look around? You saw her and—" Suddenly he stopped and grinned, his eyes crinkling at the corners. "I get it, you think there may have been a little hanky-panky going on? Kid, I wasn't even in the room. Harry Shields and I ran into each other in the lounge and, after a little fancy fencing around with each other, decided to come clean. He knew I wasn't one of the thieves; he found my credentials out in a spot check with his headquarters. So we had a little game of show and tell, and decided to join forces, but to wait them out—just in hopes we could get a line on the jewelry, too."

The dull ache in her head made it hard for Amanda to concentrate any longer. "Wynne," she said, suddenly feeling drained and weary, "I can't seem to take it in, everything happening suddenly. I can hear what you say, I saw Graham and Dianne being taken away, but it doesn't seem real, any of it."

He was on his feet, frowning. "You better rest now, Amanda. You look all bleached out. I'm going to get the room steward and have the bed made up for you, because that's where you are going!"

"Oh, no, Wynne, I don't—" she said, but it was to his back as he yanked open the door and disappeared.

Amanda leaned back against the sofa, closing her eyes. She felt mentally and physically spent. Haunting her thoughts was a crazy montage of the day's happenings—most unbelievable of all, Graham being led away. Little bits and pieces jangled together like a revolving kaleidoscope of memory: Graham, that first day on board; in the theater, holding her hand; the swift kiss he had pressed on her startled lips that night on deck. Graham, always romantic and possessive. Amanda's fingers strayed toward her neck to touch the small heart that still hung there. Then the gray-white limestone walls of the cave began to blot everything else out of her thoughts. Because that was surely Graham, too.

The steward and Wynne quickly put the room in some semblance of order, then the bed was made up for Amanda. And though she protested stubbornly, she was ordered into it by Wynne.

He frowned as he handed her a menu. "You are also going to have dinner in bed, the dining steward will bring you whatever you want."

She peered up at him over the top of the menu and started to say something, but his jaw was set firmly and he got his words in before she had a chance. "And don't argue about everything, Amanda. You tend to be obstinate and argumentative. Very bad habit you have."

Amanda looked at him steadily. "And you, Wynne Harrison, are bossy and dictatorial."

Nevertheless, however much she had protested, she was secretly glad to be exactly where she was. The thought of facing a dining room, a dinner table, with the other passengers turning questioning eyes upon her, seemed a little more than she could bear at the moment.

Thinking of Graham, let alone talking about him, was like gingerly touching a sore place. It was not that she had been in love with him, she reflected, not at all, but whatever she had thought of him, it was painful to realize what he really was like under his pleasant, romantic exterior. Had he meant to kill her? Or only stun her? Why? Why would he think she would have whatever they had wanted?

She rolled that over in her mind as the steward set the tray beside her and left. Slowly she lifted the napkin, still fretting at the question. *Why?* She had not threatened him, she was no danger to him.

When Wynne returned later to give an approving

glance at her empty tray, she asked him the same question.

"Why do you suppose Graham, and I suppose it was Graham, should suddenly decide to attack me in the cave? He'd always been friendly."

"That beats me!" He shook his head blankly. "Attack me—yes. That could make sense. Maybe he was on to me. But you? I don't see it. Did you say anything to him, anything you hadn't said before, that might have triggered the attack?"

He had pulled up the chair to sit beside her bed, making her uncomfortably conscious of his nearness and the suggested intimacy of the situation. Here she was, in bed, in her nightgown, feeling a shy embarrassment, but she might as well have been fully clothed and sitting primly clear across the room from him as far as he seemed to notice, she thought.

But he was waiting for her to answer. She reviewed his question in her mind. *Had* she said anything new to Graham? But of course she had! Without thinking, she blurted out, "Only that I was going home from Auckland ..." Her voice trailed off as she realized what she had said. She closed her mouth tightly and a little too late.

"Why?"

Amanda's mind was confused enough without having to search around in it frantically to find an answer that wouldn't betray her real reason.

"I don't mean why were you telling him that. I mean why were you planning to go home? You would have to have mentioned it at a time before I brought up the subject on the way home from the caves. A few hours ago." He was curt.

She would not meet his eyes. "I—I—" she began defensively, took a deep breath, and said simply, "because I am."

"But it's all over now. I suggested it only because I wanted to spare you knowing about Moore, but now that you do, there's no reason to go. But you had made up your mind before. Why?"

Why couldn't he stop asking that? Amanda gazed up toward the top of her bunk, at the wall, everywhere but in Wynne's direction, tightening her fingers around the top of the sheet.

"Amanda?"

"Because I wanted to, that's why! And I am going," she said unevenly, her eyelids stinging.

He paused a long moment before saying, "All right, Amanda, we can get back to that later. But, in answer to your question, that's why! Because he thought you were going home suddenly. 'Now why would she do that,' he'd ask himself, 'unless she had found it?' If he had been romancing you for the same reason Dianne had me—I'm not saying he was, but they both seemed to be anxious to ingratiate themselves—then your abrupt decision to leave must have stunned him. He had to act at once."

"He had to find out if I had it in my purse, with me?" Now Amanda did turn her head to look at Wynne.

"Right, and he probably searched you to see if you had it on you," he said levelly.

Amanda's face flamed as she recalled the unbuttoned blouse. "B-but I didn't have it."

"So he hightailed it right back here. Left the bus at the first stop, I was told, saying he was going back to help me look for you. But he took a taxi or hired a car, and kited right back to the ship and this room. And our good old flatfoot, Shields, caught him at it. Moore figured you found it, and if you didn't have it on you, it was back here for sure."

A pause. Then Wynne got right back to the question.

"Why do you want to go home, Amanda?"

It was no easier to find the answer now than before, she thought, finally resorting to a fretful shake of the head, which did her headache little good. And didn't stop Wynne.

"Something to do with Moore?"

"No," she said in desperation. "I—I didn't like him that much. He was nice, but he was too, too—" She hesitated, then added, "He came on a little too strong."

Her head was not turned in his direction now, yet she was somehow aware that he was looking at her. But he said no more on the subject.

Pushing back his chair, he stood up. "All right, Amanda Conklin, I'll make myself scarce for a while, let you get some rest. Tomorrow we've got a number of things to straighten out. Tonight, forget everything that happened, if you can. It's over."

To her amazement, she felt the swift brush of his lips on her cheek.

"You look like hell tonight, Amanda, all peaked and pale; you're as stubborn as a Missouri mule, but you're a good kid!"

With that, he was gone.

Chapter 11

As Wynne's footsteps went echoing briskly down the hall, Amanda lifted her hand to touch her cheek, not quite certain of her inner reaction. It was rather like him, she reflected, to accompany such a gesture with a teasing comment, calculated to rob it of any romantic possibility.

Propping herself up on her elbow, she gazed at her reflection in the mirror above the dressing table. He was right, she did look like hell, she thought caustically. Dark half-moons under her eyes, face drawn, her hair matted.

Lying back down, she knew that part of the strained look was due not to the accident alone, but to the whirlwind climax of the strange conspiracy of crime between Graham and Dianne, two most unlikely criminals. There were still so many unanswered questions.

For a little while she tried fretfully and uselessly to puzzle her way through the enigma, but everything in her mind grew shadowy and vague until, finally, she slept.

It was late the next morning when she awakened, opening her eyes drowsily to lift a lazy hand to push back a strand of hair drifting across her face. Her eyelids flew open wide as she touched the tender bump on her head, bringing memory flooding back. She struggled to a sitting position.

"Wynne?" she called questioningly.

There was no answer. He was up and gone, the bathroom door stood open, the faint scent of shaving lotion lingering hauntingly. It would always remind her of Wynne in the future.

She should get up, she urged herself, she should do something about packing, seeing the doctor—then leaving. Leaving. The very word left a hollow feeling inside. But she had made her decision, it was the only logical thing to do. The arrest of Dianne and Graham in no way changed the main reason for going, that of needing to get away from Wynne. It was clear that the absence of the red-haired girl wasn't going to alter her own chances.

Shoving back the covers, she started to get up, but quickly grabbed them back into place at a light tap on the door.

"Yes?" she called.

"Wynne. Don't get up, I'll let myself in." With that, a key sounded in the lock and he came in, one large glossy flower clutched stiffly in his hand. "For the invalid," he said soothingly.

He was absurd, Amanda thought, staring in some bewilderment at the artificial-looking waxy red flower thrust at her.

"I admit it doesn't look much like a sick-room bloom," he said ruefully. "But that's all they had in the dining room for decoration today. I conned this one out of our pal, the headwaiter."

"What in the world is it?" she questioned, turning it about curiously in her hand.

"I think it's called an anthurium, if I correctly remember what he said. Anyhow, I felt it only appropriate to carry a floral tribute to an invalid."

"Thank you," she replied primly, eyes amused.

"How are you feeling this morning?" he asked, stepping to the bathroom to get a toothbrush glass for the flower.

"I'm perfectly all right now," she said almost truthfully.

"Good!" He stuck the flower in the glass, then looked around at Amanda. "Now, would you like me to help you on with your robe so you can get dressed for breakfast, or would you prefer that the steward bring you something?" He had picked up her dressing gown and stood waiting.

"Put that down, Wynne Harrison," she ordered indignantly. "I can manage perfectly well. If you will have the courtesy to leave the stateroom for a few minutes."

"If you insist." He paused at the door. "I ought to warn you, there'll be questions today from the police, about the accident in the cave yesterday."

"When, do you know?" The ship sailed at four in the afternoon. She would have to hurry to be ready by then if the police were late in arriving or kept her very long.

He shrugged. "I don't know. Just that they'll be here."

A few moments later, standing in the bathroom, she was aware of the shadow that hung over her spirits. Over and over her mind replayed the scene of Graham, then Dianne, being taken off the ship in custody. She had never cared for Dianne, not really, but Graham ... she couldn't help but be sorry. True, his interest in her was no doubt for the purpose of somehow getting into the stateroom, but she almost wished he had been able to escape his captors.

Amanda had trouble, even now, realizing that he wouldn't be up on deck somewhere, strolling about, waiting for her to appear. All the rest seemed dreamlike. Only this, she touched the raised place on her head, only this made it real.

Nearly everyone had left the dining room when she got there. The headwaiter, his voice and face concerned over her well-being, led her to the empty table. Wynne followed along behind, hands in his pockets. He sat drinking coffee as she ate; he had breakfasted earlier, he told her. The deep Irish eyes were remote and unreadable.

"Anything new about Dianne and Graham? What's going to happen?" Amanda set her cup down.

He shook his head. "It'll be a get-in-line routine, I'd say, as to who gets a chance at them first. There's the initial jewel robbery, of course, the attack on you, possibly one on me, but those two might be a little harder to prove. And there's always the murder of the first crook; *that's* never been solved. Anyhow, my guess is they'll face extradition to the States."

Wynne waited a moment, then said abruptly, "Now, about you, Amanda. What's all this talk about going back to Arizona? I didn't press it last night because you weren't feeling up to much, but now I'd like an answer."

She lowered her eyes and began to carefully push her fork around after a barely visible speck of egg on her plate. "It's settled," she replied in a flat little voice. "I'm going as soon as I see the doctor and talk to whoever is coming to question me."

"I thought this trip was so terribly important to you? A sort of sentimental pilgrimage. That's the impression I got. You fought like a young wildcat for that room of ours, I didn't think anyone or anything could have changed your mind. What did?"

Amanda lifted her napkin to touch it to her lips. Her breakfast was finished, she no longer had an excuse to busy herself with food in order to avoid his eyes. So, reluctantly, she looked up.

"I've always understood it was a woman's privilege to change her mind," she said, not quite steadily. "I've changed mine."

"I see," he drawled, "which means of course that I

don't see why at all. You say it isn't because of Graham
Moore, then have I done anything to offend you? I figure
it has to be something in the unforgivable category if you
are making such a drastic decision.

She pushed back from the table, getting to her feet.
"No, nothing that you've done. If you'll excuse me, I'm
going to check with the doctor now. He said to." She gave
him a polite, strained smile as she hurried off.

If he'd just leave her alone! Stop those prying questions! Amanda went quickly up the stairs toward the
foyer, her lips pressed tight. One more word from him
and she'd have burst into tears! Right out there in the
middle of the dining room at the breakfast table! That,
she reminded herself sharply, was just precisely why she
must go. Sooner or later she'd be certain to betray herself. And how would that be—Wynne sharing a room
with someone he knew had fallen in love with him? He'd
be embarrassed, uncomfortable, maybe even irritated. He
had so cautiously detailed the limits of their relationship
at the very beginning.

The doctor nodded approvingly as he examined her.
"Fine! The bump has gone down and the lacerations are
healing nicely. However, just to be on the safe side, I
might as well take one more look at it tomorrow." He
smiled at her benignly. "That's a mighty devoted husband you have. I like to see that these days," he said as
he walked her to the door.

Tomorrow? Tomorrow, with her present plans, she'd
be in a plane and on her way to the States, Amanda
thought guiltily.

Wynne was sitting in the doctor's waiting room as she
came out. He got up and came over to her. "They're here.
The police," he said briefly, motioning with his head at an
office door across the hall. "They'd like to talk to you."

She looked inquiringly at him, hesitating.

"No," he said, getting her meaning without words.

"Just you. I've already talked to them and I'll be seeing them later with Shields when he comes back on board."

She walked slowly across the hall and into the office, the door was open. As she entered, a tall thin man spoke politely to her, asking her to take a seat, and closed the door. Two other men were sitting about a table, and they looked up as she slipped into a seat. Later, when Amanda tried to recall the interview, it all seemed to meld together in a whirl of questions, pages flipping in notebooks, the sound of footsteps passing by in the hall outside.

Had she any idea who had hit her, had it been Graham Moore? The question had come from a ruddy-cheeked policeman whose gentle voice and friendly manner did not match the sharp shrewd eyes. Amanda could only reply helplessly that she didn't *know*, it wouldn't be fair to say, for she hadn't seen her assailant. There were other questions, too, numerous ones, all most courteously put, but repeated over and over in various ways. Basically they were concerned with ferreting out everything she knew about Graham. It wasn't much. He'd not said a lot about himself really, except that he was an artist, which he probably wasn't, she supposed, and that he had traveled.

At last they allowed her to leave, thanking her and expressing their regret that she had been injured on her visit to New Zealand.

Wynne was nowhere in sight, so she went down to the stateroom to begin packing, a strange reluctance tugging at her. But she must go, she knew that, more each time she was around him. Letting herself into the empty room, she began pulling out drawers, ruefully taking out the clothes, folding them with care and placing them on the sofa.

She rang for the steward. He would have to get her

suitcases for her. At the knock on the door, she opened it, ready to ask for them. But it was Wynne.

He walked into the stateroom, turned, and glowered about at the neatly stacked clothes.

"Now, just a darned minute, Amanda Conklin. I asked you a question. Several times, if I remember correctly. And this time I'd like an answer, not one of your stubborn evasions. Last time I brought it up, you left the table in a hurry to the doctor's office. And no answer. Now, let's forget all the little vocal pirouettes and tell me what I want to know. If I've hurt your feelings, offended you unknowingly, at least allow me the chance to set things right."

Amanda nervously fingered the pink sweater she had started folding before he came in, casting about for something to say.

"You said it wasn't anything to do with Graham Moore. You still stick to that?" Wynne was impatient.

"Yes," she said carefully, laying the sweater on top of the other clothes for packing.

"Then," he snapped decisively, "it's got to be something I've managed to do, without being aware. All right, if that's the case, I've got a solution."

"And that is?"

He managed to look overpatient. "I saw the doctor a few moments before I came in here, he says he'd like to see you one more time."

"But the ship sails today."

He nodded. "That's so. Without three of our passengers." He jerked his head toward the door. "The room across from us is now vacant, due to the departure of Moore and Shields. Neither will be coming back. Dianne had a stateroom alone. Now, why don't I trot up to the purser without delay and see if I can get one of those vacancies for you—or for me, if you would allow me to

continue my search of this room in my so far fruitless
hunt?"

Amanda considered. It would still mean seeing him
about on the ship, but release her from the sweet painful
misery of their present intimacy, sleeping in the same
small room, touching him unavoidably as she brushed
past him because of the narrow space between the beds
and the dressing table.

"Well?" he prodded her with his voice.

"I—maybe—perhaps—" she began uncertainly.

"Great! Such enthusiasm! Come on, my dear little obstinate donkey, time's passing. If I'm going to make a try
for another accommodation, I'd better not waste any
moments standing here in a long-winded discussion.
There's always the chance there's a waiting list for vacancies." He thumped his fists down on his hips, gazing
at her impatiently.

A knock at the door. Wynne twisted his head.

"It's probably the steward, I was going to ask for my
suitcases," Amanda explained.

Wynne opened the door, poking his head out. "Sorry
to have bothered you, we won't need anything after all,"
he said.

Then he turned back to Amanda. "All right, I'll see
what I can do about getting you a release from my apparently objectionable presence." His voice was grim.
"Let the purser think we've had another domestic battle
and a desire for separate rooms."

Wynne mustn't feel it was all his fault, that there was
something wrong with him or his actions, she thought
disconcertedly, that wasn't fair! "No," she burst out, "you
aren't. I mean, it isn't that. It's only—only—" And there
she stuck, feeling a betraying rush of color to her face.

A pause. Then he said in a quiet voice, "That's good
to know. I wondered. Anyhow, I'll go now. It may take
a little while, so don't worry."

"But not a single room, please, Wynne, it's too expensive," she said hurriedly in a voice she was relieved to find sounded almost normal.

"Right. See what I can do." With that, he left.

Amanda stood where she was, right in the middle of the stateroom, for a full two minutes after his departure. Had she made a mistake, she wondered? Should she have decided to stay on? Well, it was a little late now to have afterthoughts.

It was nearly lunchtime when she went to the dining salon, expecting to see Wynne when he had finished arranging for the room. Only Joan was at the table, her eyes round and full of questions.

"I never cared for Dianne," she said frankly, "and if it had to be someone the police came for, I'm quite glad it was that one! I've only heard bits and pieces. Can you tell me what happened? Begin with the accident at the cave." Joan stared curiously at Amanda's head. "I heard you were hurt."

The report Amanda gave her was carefully made, revealing only the obvious, withholding Wynne's connection and personal professional interest.

"And that handsome Graham Moore!" Joan put down her teacup. "Goodness knows there are few enough left who are attractive-looking, pity he had to be a baddo."

Joan wasn't the only interested person. After leaving the luncheon table, a bit disconcerted at the nonappearance of Wynne, Amanda encountered elderly Mrs. Stewart on the way through the lounge.

The woman dragged Amanda over to a sofa, then perched beside her, bright blue eyes sparkling with excitement. "Oh, my dear," she cried, "how thrilling it must have been, not your being attacked, but to be right in the heart of a real criminal roundup! Who put the finger on them, do you know?" The thin little bird claw of a hand clasped Amanda's arm.

But she did not wait for a reply as she piled one question on top of another. "Was that red-haired girl his moll? Was she the canary, do you know?" The gray head bobbed up and down knowingly. "That means, did she sing, did she tell the fuzz about him?" The woman scrutinized Amanda searchingly. "You're not a gumshoe yourself, a private eye, are you?"

Amanda shook her head dazedly in the flow of the nonstop queries. "I really haven't much information yet, it's all so recent, it's happened so quickly," she managed to stick in between volleys of questions.

Mrs. Stewart nodded. "I know, I know," she said soothingly, "it must be trying to be a hapless victim. I was so hoping you were a private detective, like that wonderful old lady in the stories, I can't remember her name, my dear, but she was always right in the midst of the rub-outs, the capers. As I recall, she was often hit on the head just like you. I don't mean often for you, but yesterday you were."

The woman sat back, clasping her hands comfortably in her lap. "Just think of it," she said, "what a lot goes on! In the last three trips we've had a murder, at least a disappearance that was undoubtedly a murder; then an arrest on the next trip; now, on this one, we have *two* arrests, a mugging, you, my dear, though perhaps the proper term is sand-bagging. And the cruise isn't even over yet." She sighed contentedly. "I think from now on, I'll confine my travel to this line exclusively, it's so stimulating."

Amanda stole a glance at her watch and hurriedly made the truthful excuse that she had to look for Wynne. Time was fast approaching for the sailing of the ship. Where was Wynne?

Mrs. Stewart patted Amanda's hand. "You just run right along, Amanda dear, I understand perfectly. Young love!" She smiled benignly.

Wynne was not in the stateroom. Amanda worriedly made her way back up on deck, to look down on the dock where last-minute shoppers were scurrying back to the ship. Wynne was not there. Nor on the upper deck. Now she made her way again to the stateroom to sit gingerly on the edge of the sofa, her eyes on the door.

At last she heard him knock and she rose hurriedly to pull open the door. It was Wynne.

"What did you find out?" she gasped anxiously. "There isn't much time left. Did they have room for me . . . another room?"

His expression was clearly not encouraging. She was already beginning to panic as he spoke, "I'm sorry, Amanda, I've been sitting up there in the purser's office, hoping for a no-show, as they call them. They have a long list of people awaiting possible cancellations, both rooms were snapped up almost the very moment they were empty. Our only hope was to have one of those who got the rooms not to show up before we sailed."

As she opened her mouth to speak, the ship's whistle blasted, the all-ashore sounding. Amanda's eyes were stunned as she looked helplessly around the room.

"How can I possibly—there isn't time—how will I . . . ?" she gasped.

Wynne was shaking his head sadly. "I'm sorry, Amanda, I tried. I waited until the last possible minute to be certain that everyone who had claimed a room had boarded. I guess it's too late now. It's only four more days to Sydney. Why not plan to leave from there, if you insist on going?"

Amanda sank back on the sofa. "I guess I don't have much of a choice," she said defeatedly. Her mind seemed to be running around frantically, trying to close all gates. She'd thought it was over, now she'd have to start all over again, fighting not to let him guess.

"Well," he said cheerfully now, "we'll just have to

make the best of it, I imagine. I promise to try not to offend you in these next four days. Every moment not spent in sleeping, I shall devote to the task of discovering the object that most certainly still remains in this room. I shall endeavor not to get in your way." His voice was just a shade too innocent.

Amanda shot him a quick searching look, but his face was bland, his manner placid.

"Very well, as you say, we'll just have to make the best of it." She began putting her clothes away in the drawer.

Though her back was to him now, she was aware he was regarding her silently. She would have given anything to know what was going on in that mind of his. Wynne Harrison was an enigma in so many ways.

After a few more seconds of quiet, he said, "Well, that's that, I guess."

"Harry Shields will go on back to the States now?" she asked over her shoulder.

"Yes. His job was to seek out and nab the thieves as soon as he was certain, then, if he could, round up the jewels. If I find the clue to the cache, better make that *when*, it better not be *if*, then I'll get in touch with him right away. The jewels don't belong to my company; we just don't want to be stuck with paying the insurance."

"I can't help feeling sorry about Graham and Dianne. They don't seem the type to be criminals," she said thoughtfully, as she closed a drawer and opened another.

"Who knows what the type is?" he asked idly. "Who'd take Shields for a cop, for that matter? Not looking the type is probably the best insurance for either of those two categories.

"Well, see you around dinnertime," he said and opened the door to leave.

After he'd gone, Amanda halted what she was doing,

her hands still, the drawer gaping open. Four days.
Could she do it? Why not? she asked herself. She had
managed to get through a lot more than that without his
finding out. She would not take a single chance: she
would not dance with him, thankfully there'd be no
more stops before Australia where they'd perhaps be
alone. She would spend as little time in this room with
him as she could possibly manage. She found herself
nodding in approval.

At dinner, the Babcocks were eager to hear every de-
tail of what Lee Babcock insisted on calling the Great
South Pacific Caper. This time, Amanda was spared, for
Wynne fielded the questions adroitly, answering without
once touching the verboten areas.

The empty chair at the table, where Dianne had sat,
was a vivid reminder of her part in what had happened.

Tina Babcock nodded wisely. "There was something
about her, right from the first, that I didn't trust. I can't
tell you what it was, but it was there." She popped a
small olive in her mouth and reached for a slender stick
of celery.

"That's what I told Amanda at luncheon," Joan said
stoutly. "You'd only to see her all mockered-up in those
slinky low-cut clothes, those made-up eyes even at the
breakfast table, you know she wasn't a good type."

Wynne and Lee grinned at each other. "Women!" Lee
said, winking at Wynne.

Amanda said nothing about Dianne. How she felt
about her was something quite different from the other
two girls' reaction. She viewed Dianne in relationship to
Wynne.

After dinner, Wynne quietly absented himself to do
his continuing if unproductive search of the stateroom.
Amanda stayed away from 224 as long as she could, in
order not to be there while he was. When he came strolling into the lounge later on, she felt free to leave. None

of their friends was about, no one would notice she and Wynne were together very little.

It was no easier to spend the long night hours, so very little distance from the sleeping Wynne, no easier than it had ever been. The time will go quickly now, she whispered valiantly to herself. Only a few more days ... and nights.

Wynne was gone when she arose and began dressing the next morning. After brushing her hair and scrutinizing her makeup in the bathroom mirror, she opened the door to go back into the other room.

There was Wynne. She stared at him. He was dressed quite formally for early morning, suit, tie, and his hair had been slicked back with water, but was now springing stubborn tendrils here and there. He sat stiffly in the chair, another of those strange artificial-looking anthuriums clutched tightly in his hands.

He looks exactly like a late-nineteenth-century dandy, she thought! But what? Why?

"I," he announced solemnly, "have come courting."

Chapter 12

Amanda blinked unbelievingly. "You've what?" she gasped. Then the combination of days of tension and strain, coupled with this absurd spectacle in front of her, snapped her control and she collapsed in a torrent of giggles that grew into shaking laughter until she had to lean against the wall weakly.

"You're—you're—" She tried to speak but just looking at Wynne in that stiff formal pose, the one stark leafless flower clasped so straight and rigid in front of him, so much an old-fashioned tintype portrait come to life, sent her off into another gale of amusement.

"That's a fine attitude, I must say." He was the image of injured dignity.

Amanda was wiping away tears of mirth. "I'm sorry," she gasped breathlessly. "I really am, but after—after all that's been happening, I suppose it was the exact comedy relief I needed." She eyed him curiously. "Do you mind telling me what this is all about? Why you are dressed this way so early in the morning, as if you were about to attend a board meeting? And what was that statement of yours supposed to mean?"

He relaxed his pose to grin at her. "Thought that should help unstarch you. You've been so restrained, tense, not to say out-and-out stuffy, I had to think of something."

"All right, you have," Amanda said, her poise recovered.

He got to his feet, laying the flower on the dressing table. "Just a minute, Miss Conklin"—he held out a restraining hand as she started toward the door and breakfast—"it's not all in fun. I meant what I said."

Halting abruptly, she stared at him. Was this just more of his joke, she wondered? But, no, amusement had gone from his eyes and his words sounded serious.

"You mean . . . what?" she asked uncertainly, afraid to think what she wanted to think.

"That I'm formally announcing my honorable intentions," he said, a half-smile back on his lips. "Up until now, I've thought all your interest was on Graham Moore. I was afraid to make a move. Besides—"

"Besides, you told me that I wasn't your type," she spoke tartly, but her heart was racing.

He had the grace to look embarrassed, Amanda thought. She could see a faint tinge of red at his neckline.

"Well, what did you expect?" he asked indignantly. "Right off the bat, that very first day, you had that apprehensive look, as if you were fearful of facing a fate worse than death, as the Victorian novelists so often and incorrectly expressed it. I had to reassure you. Maybe I overdid it."

She made no answer, the tumult inside her making it impossible to think straight, let alone speak with any calmness or sense. She searched his face for a long moment.

"Are you actually serious?" she finally managed to blurt out.

"I am. I realize that our situation presents a number of hazards for a formal wooing, too many mine fields, you might say. But, Amanda"—he gripped her arm tightly—"I promise you, it'll be as circumspect and old-fashioned a wooing as I can manage, considering the extreme temptations that may present themselves."

Amanda frantically tried to think of something to say but failed, coming up only with a disjointed "I—you—but—"

"Look at me," he spoke levelly now, eyes meeting hers in a way that shook and held her. "I'll not rush you. Don't think I don't realize . . . that I'm not aware of what disadvantages there are in our situation. That it may put you on the defensive. But all I can say is, trust me, Amanda. What I'm talking about is the same chance I'd have if I met you on deck, if we weren't together in the same stateroom. Okay?"

"All right, Wynne," she said in a soft small voice.

She saw a muscle twitch at the corner of his mouth, then he drew her gently into his arms, his voice husky against her hair. "We're starting all over, Amanda, right from the very beginning, as if we'd just met."

She stirred slightly. "We're a little friendly if you consider we've just met." She lifted her head to look up at him. "I don't usually say 'How do you do?' from the circle of someone's arms." Her voice was a shade unsteady.

"I should hope not! But, I promised you, and I'll keep my promise, I won't rush you." He pulled back slightly. "I won't even kiss you now, if you say not."

She lowered her eyelashes, hiding the sudden sparkle in her eyes. "I—I don't mind," she said primly. "One."

"I'll keep it friendly—if I can," he murmured as, with a finger, he lifted her chin to tilt her head. His lips came down gently on hers, the touch cool, firm, spinning her heart and senses. For an instant there was a spark that almost got away. For an instant the kiss lost its decorous, chaste contact, turning into something that sent the blood hotly surging through Amanda's veins, before Wynne drew back abruptly. Voice husky, he said, "We'll have to watch it, Amanda. It's not going to be as easy to be circumspect as I thought."

"I can tell that, too," she said, her tone not quite normal, either. This was not real, she kept reminding herself. After the way she had so long felt secretly about Wynne, to have him say, now, even in that bantering way, that he was courting her—it was almost too much to take in all at once. But that kiss—she drew an unsteady breath—that was real!

How strange, she thought suddenly, how strange and somehow wonderful: this trip, which once had meant so very much to her mother and father, brought them so much happiness and joyous memories, was coming to mean the same thing to her—if only in a different way. For a moment their faces rose in her mind, then slowly drifted away, leaving her knowing there was one thing she had to make clear to Wynne.

"Wynne," she began, "it's—it's got to be the way you said. What I mean is, I'm not the type for these meaningful or unstructured relationships, and with the way things are, I mean our being in the same room—" She floundered and her voice trailed off.

"Don't worry, Amanda. Trust me." He hesitated, then said, "No, now that I think of it, don't trust me, keep me in line. You have to. Despite my puritanical statement a moment ago, I found out just from that one plain unadorned kiss, a bonfire is awfully easy to light." A rueful grin twisted his mouth. "But I'll try, Amanda, I'll try. Just promise me one thing."

"And that is?"

"It'll only work for us if there isn't any pressure, any rush for time. I don't want you to get off in Sydney. If you ask me, I think we owe it to each other to find out just how serious we actually are. Four days is too short, Amanda."

"But, Wynne," she said suddenly, as a thought struck

her, "what about what you're supposed to find? If you should locate it any day now, then . . . ?"

He hesitated. "Right. Then I'll have to get off at the next port. Whatever my personal feelings are, that has to come first. I'm still searching, I'll go on searching. I've got to find it. But let's play it all by ear. Stay on, please, give me a chance, as long as possible."

The reason for going had vanished. It was all right now to care about him cautiously, a little too easy to care about him—wrecklessly. He was right. They owed it to themselves to discover how serious they were.

"All right, Wynne, I'll stay on," she said simply. She felt blissfully, deliriously happy.

It showed. At lunchtime Tina Babcock eyed her cautiously. "You know, there's something different about you today, Amanda. Don't tell me getting hit on the head is the secret formula for radiance." Tina slid her a significant look, and lowering her voice, said, "I know one thing that gives a woman that inner glow. You're not . . . ?" She tilted an eyebrow quizzically.

Amanda flushed hotly. "Oh, no!"

Tina shrugged. "Well, I just wondered." Then the conversation became general and Amanda breathed a sigh of relief.

After the doctor had examined her for the final time and could release her from further care, Amanda made her way down to the stateroom to buckle on her life jacket for the routine boat drill that took place after leaving each large port. Wynne's jacket was gone, so she knew he had already gone up on deck. As she opened a dresser drawer to get her sunglasses, she saw the small heart given to her by Graham.

She lifted it in her hand to gaze down at it for a moment, a touch of sadness wrenching in her heart. She could not associate the Graham she had known with the criminal he no doubt was. The thought brought her

sharply up against the fact of the attack in the cave
and— Her eyes were drawn toward the faint dark spot
on the carpet. The cave—that had more than likely been
Graham. The murder . . . ? She turned her eyes away
from the spot quickly and put the heart back in the
drawer. That was something she did not like to think
about. Though he may not have done it, he was part of
the criminal gang that had.

Amanda shut the stateroom door behind her and went
up to join Wynne on deck.

But the days, and the nights, to come, were far from
simple or free from problems. How scrupulously careful
they became about being in their room alone more than
necessary, Amanda realized. The knock on the door was
always followed by a longer wait before inserting the
key and entering so as to have no accidental recurrence
of the day when she had been interrupted in her rush
across the room for her bathing suit. Nor did she wish to
startle him again coming out of the bathroom, wrapped
in a towel as he had that first day. After lights were out
at night, their room became unavoidably intimate in
feel. Their conversations, sometimes murmured sleepily,
coming from the upper and lower bunks, seemed as personal as the touch of a hand, the brushing of lips.

But Wynne valiantly kept to his word, trying as well
as he could to make it a regular romantic courtship.
They sat out on deck, their hands locked together; they
strolled about in the moonlight; they grinned at each
other as they made dates to go down to the movie in the
ship's theater. Their kisses were exchanged in the
shadows of the deck, never again in the giddy privacy of
their room.

On the night before they landed in Sydney, they were
on deck, the moonlight incredibly beautiful in its silver
pattern on the water. They were standing on the rail
when Wynne turned to Amanda to draw her into his

arms, pressing her close to him. Their kiss caught fire, and Amanda found herself responding to the warmth of his lips in a manner that thudded her heart and sent a sweet aching through her being.

"Humph! I told you, Claude, those two aren't married! See, carrying on like that right out here in public. Look at him, kissing her." Mrs. Hildebrand's voice shattered the beauty of the moment. "She had her arms around him, kissing him right back, brazen as you please. I tell you, it's easy to see they aren't married or they wouldn't be acting like that, don't you agree, Claude?"

"Well, now, Gertrude, I don't know, maybe they ..." her husband's hesitant voice ventured.

"Claude!"

"Oh, you're right, absolutely, Gertrude," he said hurriedly as the two of them walked on.

"Don't let her bother you, Amanda," Wynne spoke quietly. "She's a shrewish old woman who can't bear to see others who are happy or enjoying themselves."

There was, Amanda supposed, some truth in his statement, yet there was equal truth in Mrs. Hildebrand's stubborn insistence that she and Wynne were not married.

The delicate emotional spell was broken, however, so Wynne and Amanda wandered about on deck, talking about their stop in Australia the next day, about being sorry to lose Joan from their dinner table, about almost everything; by mutual unspoken consent, they avoided further reference to Mrs. Hildebrand's acid comment.

They said good-bye to Joan when the ship docked, the ruddy-cheeked Australian girl dressed rather formally for departure, wearing a checked woolen suit instead of the casual outfits she'd worn all during the trip. She bade them an almost tearful farewell, then left, going down the gangway to be immediately engulfed by a cluster of hearty relatives who had come to meet her.

"Joan's all right." Wynne nodded approval as he and Amanda watched from the ship's rail. Then he turned back to Amanda, saying reluctantly, "I'm going to have to desert you today. Contacts in town. Maybe I'll get back in time to join you on one of the tours of the city. But don't wait, I may not." He put out a hand to cover hers. "How about letting me treat you to a tour. I know you have to figure pretty close."

Amanda shook her head. "Thanks, but no. I've allowed for the short tours, I planned on them." Somehow it was important for her to maintain her independence; she couldn't explain it, even to herself.

Amanda saw Sydney, the long white beaches, the traffic-fretted city, the traces of long-ago England that still lingered over some of the buildings and crooked streets. But she missed Wynne. It was almost with relief that she faced the next day's sailing, knowing they would be together again on the ship.

When the departure time did arrive, there was something about Wynne's eyes that disconcerted her as they pulled away from the dock, leaving beautiful Sydney harbor in their wake.

He turned to her. "Let's go"—he looked around—"up there, way up on the top deck, away from everyone. I've something to say to you."

Taking her arm, he steered her up the steps, and on up to the smaller, open-deck area. There was no one about.

He turned her about to face him. "All right now, I think it is time to begin Stage Two, Amanda. Have I conducted my courtship with proper demeanor? Have I given you adequate time to consider whether or not we are really serious about each other?"

Lightning thoughts flashed through her mind. There

had been three days of sea travel from Auckland, adding that to these two days in Sydney, five days in all? Five days since he had sat there in their stateroom, clutching that ridiculous flower and saying he had come courting? She started to say something, hesitated, then said nothing. His voice had a faint amused tone, but the blue eyes looking down at her were serious.

Reaching into his jacket pocket, he brought out a small blue box, never taking his gaze from her. "Phase Two," he announced, handing it to her.

Amanda's hands trembled as she lifted the velvet lid. Then her eyes widened. She turned a questioning look at him.

He nodded. "Shall I do it right? The deck is a bit damp, otherwise I'd get down on one knee. But, if you insist—" Suddenly the grin burst forth and he started to bend.

"No, no," Amanda protested hurriedly. "Don't. It's all right, but, Wynne . . ."

"I hope you don't believe in long engagements, Amanda," he said, breaking into her disjointed sentence as he slipped the ring on her finger.

This time she could make no reply, her lips being otherwise involved at the moment. As Wynne released her a few seconds later, she murmured unsteadily, "I think I said yes, if you were asking me to marry you. At least, I meant to. And as for long or short engagements . . ." She paused to look down in half-disbelief at the ring sparkling on her finger.

"What I had in mind for one lasting the proper length of time, would be from here to Fiji," he interjected smoothly.

Startled, she gasped. "But, Wynne, that's only four days from now!"

"I," he said loftily, "don't believe in long engagements!"

"But, Wynne, it's so soon, I—I—" She floundered. Of course she loved him, of course she wanted to marry him, she reminded herself fiercely, but it was all so new. She swallowed once, hard.

"Amanda!" His voice was peremptory.

She lifted her head.

"Amanda?" Now he spoke gently, persuasively.

"I guess I don't believe in long engagements either, Wynne," she said meekly.

For the next three days and nights—especially nights—they were newly and more rigidly circumspect. Among their shipboard acquaintances, they could not overdisplay their new happiness, lest it betray them. In their room—alone—they might betray themselves.

Even Amanda's engagement ring had to be relegated to a secret and unostentatious hiding place, a thin gold chain that hung about her neck, under her dress. Its sudden display might invite curiosity.

At last the distant shore of Fiji came into view over the bow of their ship, and Amanda felt like champagne was bubbling through her veins. It was incredible, all that had happened in so short a time, incredible and wonderful. Her one small regret was that she could not ask Tina Babcock to be her matron of honor.

"Ready?" Wynne appeared at the stateroom door as the ship began pressing into the small dock.

She nodded. Picking up her purse, her dark glasses, she smiled at him. "Ready, Wynne."

The summer heat was direct and nearly overpowering at first when they emerged from the air-conditioned ship to go down the gangway. Languid merchants sat wearily fanning themselves alongside the small stalls that lined the street into town. They made token efforts to stir themselves by offering strings of shell beads or carved dolls to passersby. Amanda shook her head politely in refusal as a young woman dangled a shell bracelet invitingly. As she and Wynne made their way into town, Amanda was charmed by the warm friendliness and dignity of the handsome Fijian people.

"First things first, now!" Wynne smiled down at her. "Let's find someone who looks official and see how we go about arranging for a marriage."

"The bride's ready," Amanda said happily.

Coming down the street toward them was a broad-shouldered Fijian wearing a *sulu*, the crisp, white, notched-hemline skirt, and the navy-blue shirt and black leather sandals of the Fiji policeman.

Wynne stopped him to inquire where they could get the information they were seeking. The policeman listened gravely, then indicated a building some distance away. After making certain they had the directions in mind clearly, he bowed courteously before continuing on his way.

When Amanda and Wynne reached the proper office, the official was polite. There was nothing he could do, he said regretfully. They had not brought an American certificate with them, a marriage license from their own country? That was a pity, it would be simple if they had. But, otherwise, not in one day, no. He shrugged his shoulders helplessly. With the ship leaving tomorrow, it could not be done. There were too many necessary legal details, what Americans call red tape, he explained.

They walked slowly out into the sunshine and on down the street. For a few moments neither of them spoke.

Finally Wynne said slowly, "I'm not sure if ship's captains still have the authority to perform marriages. If so, under ordinary circumstances we could ask him to do it, but I guess ours isn't your ordinary circumstance."

"No," Amanda said in a small miserable voice, "because he thinks we already *are* married." The day was abruptly less bright and she was conscious only of the heat. The happy glow seemed to have gone out of everything. Maybe, she thought bitterly, maybe they weren't meant to get married. Maybe the Fates were stepping in to.arrange their lives.

"It looks like we'll have to postpone it until Hawaii," Wynne said. "I know we can arrange for it there. A friend of mine was married there. All you need is a blood test, then there's no waiting period between obtaining the license and the wedding itself. Sorry about this, Amanda, sorry as hell!"

"That's all right, Wynne. Hawaii isn't that far. And it might be best to have a long engagement—like five or six more days." Her brave effort at a smile wobbled at the edges.

"It's damned disappointing, to put it mildly, but let's not let it completely ruin our brief visit in Fiji," Wynne said, taking her arm. "It's beautiful country. Let's take a launch to one of the small islands that surround the place and treat ourselves to the *yaqona* ceremony. I told you about the native drink, so I think you ought to have a chance to try it. It's a required part of any Fijian tour."

An hour later, Amanda was raising her eyes from over the top of a half-coconut. "It doesn't look like anything, Wynne, just watery," she said doubtfully, peering again down at the liquid in the coconut shell.

"You haven't been to Fiji until you've had some *yaqona*," he said sternly. "It's perfectly harmless; besides, the man is looking at you, waiting."

Amanda turned her eyes toward the dark-skinned man who squatted sedately on the ground in front of her, his grass skirt crisp against the green of the turf about him. In front of him was a large hollowed-out wooden bowl. The preparing of the pale liquid had been ceremonious and involved.

Lifting the shell, she quickly swallowed the few

mouthfuls, accompanied by the sharp clap of hands and the cry of *maca* from the Fijians.

Uncertainly she lowered the shell, bowed her head in quick thanks, and stepped back to allow others to participate. Wynne was grinning at her.

"Well?" he asked.

"It's sort of—sort of—" She halted, unsure of what she could say that would describe the taste.

"Now, don't tell me it tastes like muddy water, that's what everyone says," he warned her.

"Well, it does," she said stoutly. That was exactly it.

"Maybe it's an acquired taste. Anyhow, if anyone should ever ask you if you ever tried *yaqona* in Fiji, you can say yes. But, Amanda," his voice was suddenly serious, "what I'd really planned on was champagne, to toast our wedding day."

At that, they both fell silent. Then they changed the conversation forcefully and somehow the day was gotten through.

Chapter 13

The next morning, after the boat had sailed from Fiji, Wynne set about his usual frustrating search. Amanda sat in the chair, watching him. He prodded at the edge of the carpeting with a nail file, slipping the blade down between the fabric and the wall, sliding it along.

"He can't have pried up the rug to hide it," Wynne said glumly, "that would have damaged the material, left signs." He settled back on his heels. "But there's nothing along here, either. Where is it, Amanda? Give me an idea. I've flogged my brain until it's limp. The darned thing's not here! Yet ... it is! I know it is. My boss knows it. Dianne and Graham, as well as the guy arrested earlier, they all know it."

With her eyes, Amanda scanned the walls, the floor, the ceiling. But she had done that before. Lowering her gaze, she looked at Wynne's discouraged face.

"Every place I can think of, you've tried," she said. "Not once, but over and over. What's going to happen when you get back, if you haven't found it?"

"My boss is going to be plenty sore. Sure, he was all graciousness when he offered me the trip. 'Great vacation, Harrison, you deserve a rest, you've been working hard!' His exact words. But that little rider he added about looking for something that was important"— Wynne grinned ruefully—"that was the big ball of wax, as they say. And he's going to give me a hard look and' words to match if I come home without it."

He stood up. "I'll leave it for now, it's almost time for our regular boat drill. Afterward, I'm coming right back to have another look. And another. Oh, the fiendishness of inanimate objects!" His jaw set stubbornly.

At the clanging of the warning bell signaling the drill, Amanda got to her feet, went over to the small wall closet that housed the life jackets, and dragged hers out, buckling it about her obediently. As Wynne was donning his, Amanda abruptly halted, her attention on the bright-orange-canvas jacket, a startling idea bursting inside her mind.

"Wynne!" Her heart knocked against her ribs in excitement. "Wynne, I just thought. Could it be that he put it"—her eyes were intercepted by his, suddenly alert—"the life jackets, Wynne?"

He was shaking his head. "Sorry, Amanda. One of the first things I inspected. *And* the cabinet where they are kept. I checked both jackets."

Her spirits plummeted. For a moment she had hoped she had found the answer that troubled him. Then she sighed and joined Wynne in the hallway.

Out on deck, the wind blowing briskly, carrying the heavy warmth of the tropical heat away, Wynne and Amanda stood with the other passengers as the routine instructions of the drill were repeated; then at the ending signal, they trooped back to their stateroom and began unbuckling the jackets to store them in their closet.

Amanda's hand lingered on the canvas strap, her eyes thoughtful. Then, looking down, she traced the stitching at one side of the jacket with her fingernail.

"Still not convinced?" Wynne's voice brought her eyes up. "I know the feeling, Amanda, I've had it over and over, about every single place, every single possibility in the whole room."

"What did he do—that man, Desmond, the man who was killed, the one you think hid whatever it was? For a living, I mean?" she asked, her mouth suddenly drying nervously.

"Do? He was a professional criminal, Amanda. That's about his total career, or so his record reads. Why?" There was a new sharpness in his tone, a tensing. Amanda realized instinctively that this was a Wynne she didn't know, the investigator, the inflexible hunter of facts or men.

"Was he ever a tailor?" Her fingers still trailed along the edge of the jacket.

The tightness in his shoulders and his voice relaxed. "For a minute, I thought, well, I don't quite know what I thought, but to answer your question, I don't know. If you are thinking he ripped open the jacket to put something in it, I looked, first thing. I couldn't see a single sign of anything at all. It looks untouched. Both jackets, in fact."

"But, Wynne, if he ever was a tailor, or if he worked at that trade while he was in prison," she said stubbornly, "he could have opened a seam and put something inside, then sewed it up again so that the ordinary person would never know."

"But I looked, Amanda, thoroughly," he said reluctantly, still holding his own jacket, turning it over slowly in his hands.

"If you say it isn't anywhere else that you know of, then couldn't it be that he was expert enough with a needle so that you wouldn't know?"

For a moment he didn't answer, but stood there, a remote expression on his face. Then he brought his attention back to Amanda, a blue fire beginning to light in the depths of the Irish eyes.

"I wonder," he said, "I wonder." He scrutinized his jacket, seam by seam. Then he shook his head. "If he did that, he's got to be an expert. Mind if I look at yours again?" He held out his hand.

She handed it over to him as he examined it with the same detailed care, but with little optimism.

He tossed both jackets on the sofa and reached into his pocket for a knife. Unfolding it, he looked up at Amanda.

"Well, here goes. I have a feeling my firm is going to owe the shipping line for two jackets. But I haven't any better ideas to offer."

Amanda's heart again began bumping uncomfortably inside her chest as Wynne lifted one of the jackets, set it on the dressing table, and began carefully cutting the threads at one of the seams. Moments later, the outer covering was laid back, exposing the inner padding—and nothing else.

The room felt uncomfortably still. "I'm sorry, Wynne, I thought it might be there," she said in a small apologetic voice that was barely audible.

"Cheer up, we still have one to go," Wynne said encouragingly if not particularly optimistically.

She watched as the small knife went slitting through the seam on one side, then he lifted the jacket to turn it around.

There was a light metallic tinkle as something hit the top of the dressing table. The orange-canvas life jacket slid unnoticed from Wynne's grasp to the floor, as he picked up a small flat key from the dresser.

"It's it, my God, it's it!" His voice was unbelieving. Then he turned swiftly and grabbed Amanda, hugging her fiercely. "You're a marvel, Amanda darling, a wonderful marvel!"

After a few seconds of jubilation, he turned over the key in his hand. "A locker key, an ordinary airport locker key, and it's got the name of the city stamped into it. Our luck was all bad, now it's all good."

He started to pull away from Amanda, then gave her another exuberant hug and said, "I hate to leave you, but I've got to get on the radio telephone without delay and get word to the boss. He'll be out of his skull with relief. This little object"—he dangled it in front of her— "thanks to you, is going to save our company a small fortune."

"There's no doubt that this is it—what you were looking for," she asked nervously.

"Not one in the world," he said positively. "It all ties in neatly."

With that, he left, heading in a hurry toward the ship's radio-telephone operator's office.

The sweet haunting strains of "Aloha Oe" floated on the soft evening air, serpentine uncurled from the ship's railing down onto the dock, as the cruise ship gave one last blast of its whistle and began to pull away from Honolulu, accompanied by cries of farewell from those onshore.

Amanda and Wynne stood arm in arm, leaning over the rail, smiling and waving at no one in particular. He turned to her. "Amanda, or may I call you Mrs. Harrison now? How do you like married life?"

Her eyes sparkled up at him. "Speaking from the long experience of four hours and thirty-five minutes, I'd say it's not all that bad."

"I've got to hand it to my boss," Wynne said. "He came through for me. He was so darned relieved to get the case tied up that he was actually willing to send a courier to pick up the key in Honolulu and let me complete the trip by ship. That's got to be an all-time high for the old man. I had to lean on him a little, and he agreed to it grudgingly, but he did it."

The moonlight patterned across the deck as the ship swept softly through the darkened water. Wynne yawned elaborately. "I suppose it's about time to call it a day, a long day, but an unforgettable one. Which reminds me, we've got one more thing to settle."

"And that is ... ?" She tilted her head questioningly.

"Well, I don't like to complain, but the altitude of my upper bunk is beginning to bother me. So I wonder if tonight, I might presume ... ?"

"You may," she said demurely, as they left the deck and went in through the door.

As they passed through the lounge, Mrs. Stewart was coming toward them with another woman. They stopped to speak to Amanda and Wynne for a few minutes, chatting cheerfully about Honolulu, then went on.

"Did you notice"—Mrs. Stewart bent her head to one side to speak to her friend—"Amanda has decided to wear her wedding ring. I'm so glad."

Big Bestsellers from SIGNET

☐ **ROGUE'S MISTRESS by Constance Gluyas.**
(#J7533—$1.95)

☐ **SAVAGE EDEN by Constance Gluyas.** (#J7171—$1.95)

☐ **LOVE SONG by Adam Kennedy.** (#E7535—$1.75)

☐ **THE DREAM'S ON ME by Dotson Rader.**
(#E7536—$1.75)

☐ **SINATRA by Earl Wilson.** (#E7487—$2.25)

☐ **SUMMER STATION by Maud Lang.** (#E7489—$1.75)

☐ **THE WATSONS by Jane Austen and John Coates.**
(#J7522—$1.95)

☐ **SANDITON by Jane Austen and Another Lady.**
(#J6945—$1.95)

☐ **THE FIRES OF GLENLOCHY by Constance Heaven.**
(#E7452—$1.75)

☐ **A PLACE OF STONES by Constance Heaven.**
(#W7046—$1.50)

☐ **THE ROCKEFELLERS by Peter Collier and David Horo-**
witz. (#E7451—$2.75)

☐ **THE HAZARDS OF BEING MALE by Herb Goldberg.**
(#E7359—$1.75)

☐ **COME LIVE MY LIFE by Robert H. Rimmer.**
(#J7421—$1.95)

☐ **KINFLICKS by Lisa Alther.** (#E7390—$2.25)

☐ **RIVER RISING by Jessica North.** (#E7391—$1.75)

THE NEW AMERICAN LIBRARY, INC.,
P.O. Box 999, Bergenfield, New Jersey 07621

Please send me the SIGNET BOOKS I have checked above. I am
enclosing $_____(check or money order—no currency
or C.O.D.'s). Please include the list price plus 35¢ a copy to cover
handling and mailing costs. (Prices and numbers are subject to
change without notice.)

Name_____

Address_____

City_____State_____Zip Code_____
Allow at least 4 weeks for delivery